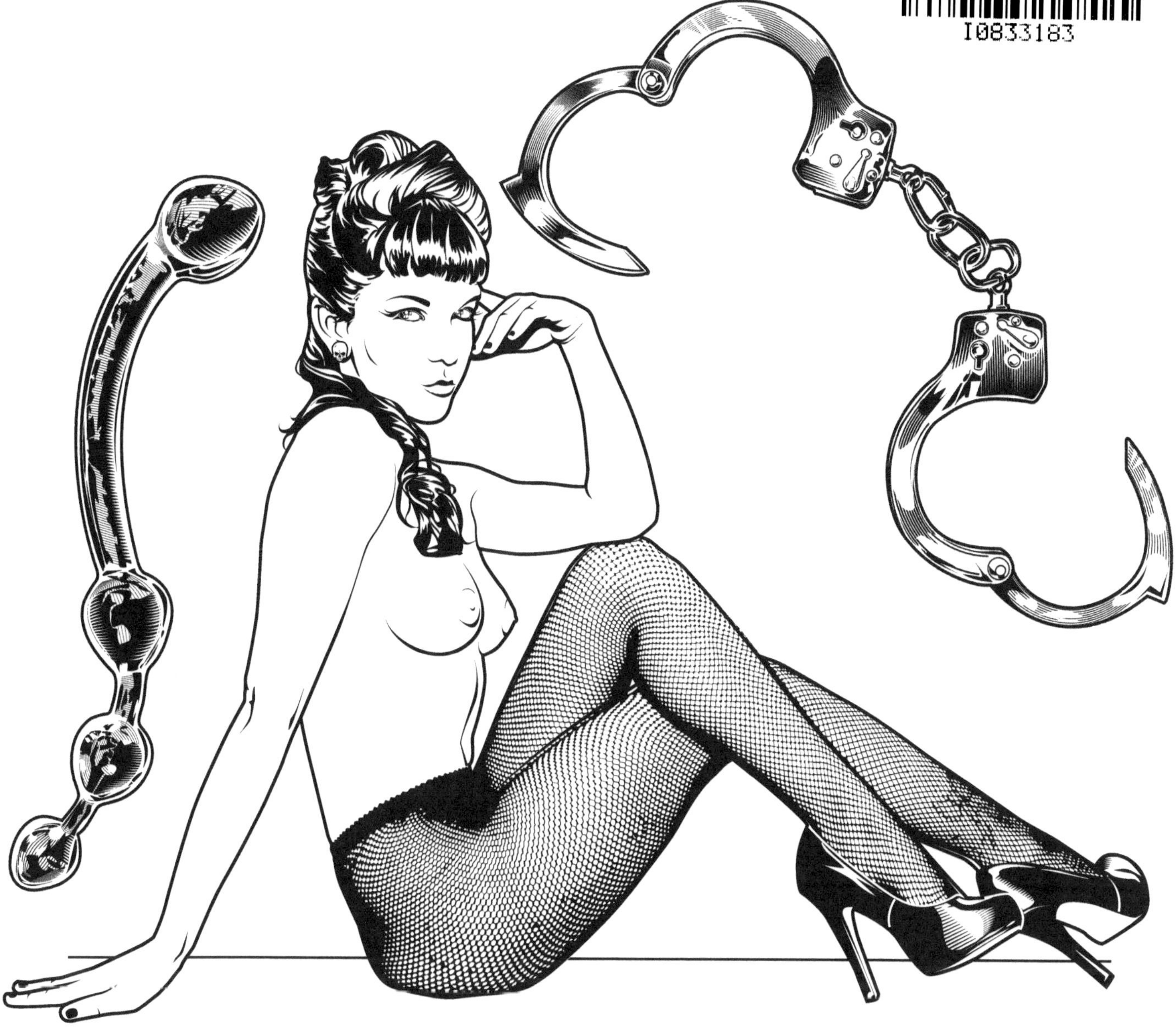

THE KINKY COLORING BOOK

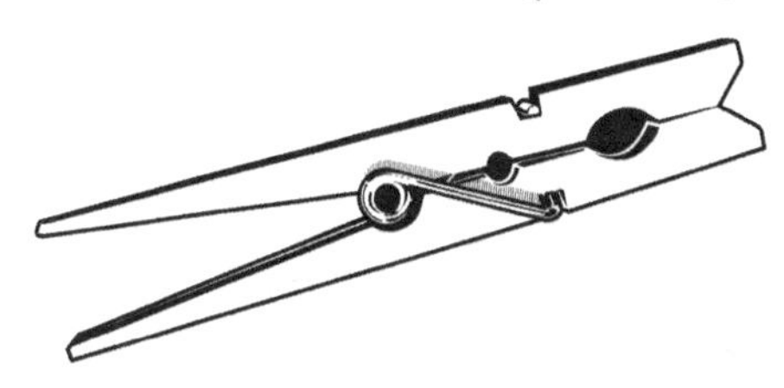

BY JAMES COURTNEY

The Kinky Coloring Book
By James Courtney

ISBN 978-0-9858999-0-5

Dedicated to Jeff Cathcart

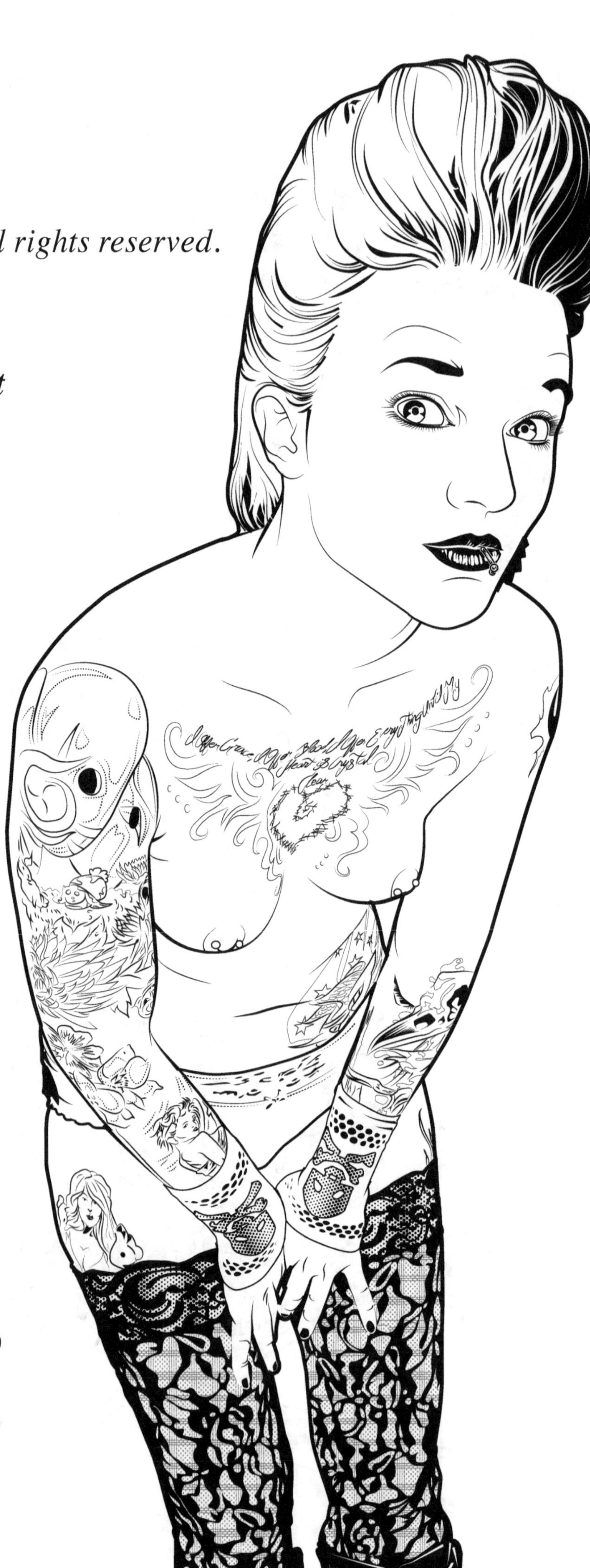

Nakedcomix.com
James Courtney
793 South Tracy Blvd #210
Tracy CA., 95376

In making the art for The Kinky Coloring Book, I have had the privilege of working with some very talented and generous people. I'd like to take a moment to thank some that have helped me to deliver this project into your hands.

Owen Johnson and the Cyber-Dyke Network, have been a supporter of me and Nakedcomix since the beginning. Without his generosity, I doubt that I would be able to have gotten this far.

Jeff Cathcart and Treja Hayes have both helped me behind (and sometime in front) of the camera almost from the start. They have both contribuated to my artistic vision with their own hard work and talents. I feel blessed to have such good friends at my side.

I'd like to thank Mariah Carle, Kathryn Kaminski and Megu for their gift of studio space and time. As well as putting up with naked models getting spattered with paint or fake blood or generally making a mess of their nice, clean work spaces.

My various make-up artists, Treja Hayes, Justina Downs, Tasha Lopez, Dee Dee Leiter and Daniella. They have all worked hard to make my models look good, and as a result, made me look good. I can't imagine doing a photo shoot without them.

Penny McClish of Lust Design for modeling and loaning me her latex creations for a couple of shoots. CorruptMorals for his generosity and great rigging skills, also for his willingness to step in front of the camera a couple of times too. The Wicked Grounds Cafe and the San Francisco Citadel for hosting two of my very first shows. Sharon Cathcart for her text editing help. Amy Kee Aifd for her marketing advice. Sandra Chang, Dustin Adair, Meg Valentine and Lee Nisbet for their moral support over the years.

Finally, I'd like to thank all the models I have worked with over the years. It is no small thing to be able to take off your clothes and step in front of the camera. It takes nerve, and I consider it a gift to have worked with you all. Thank you.

James Courtney
Nakedcomix.com

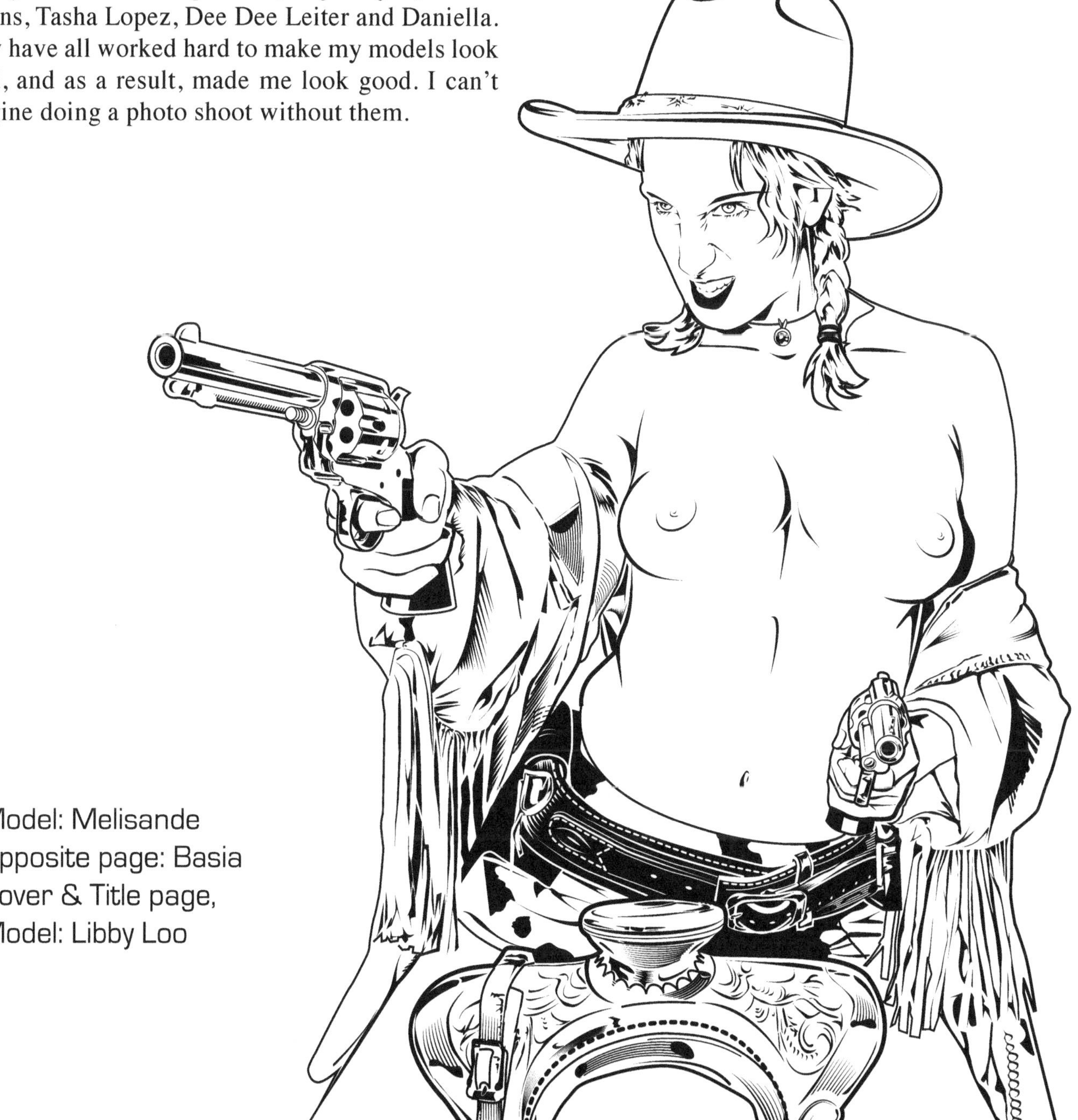

Model: Melisande
Opposite page: Basia
Cover & Title page,
Model: Libby Loo

WARNING: When Lyssa asks you if you'd babysit her kids on date night, remember she doesn't take "no" very well.

Bad Decisions

Model: Mellissa Yvette

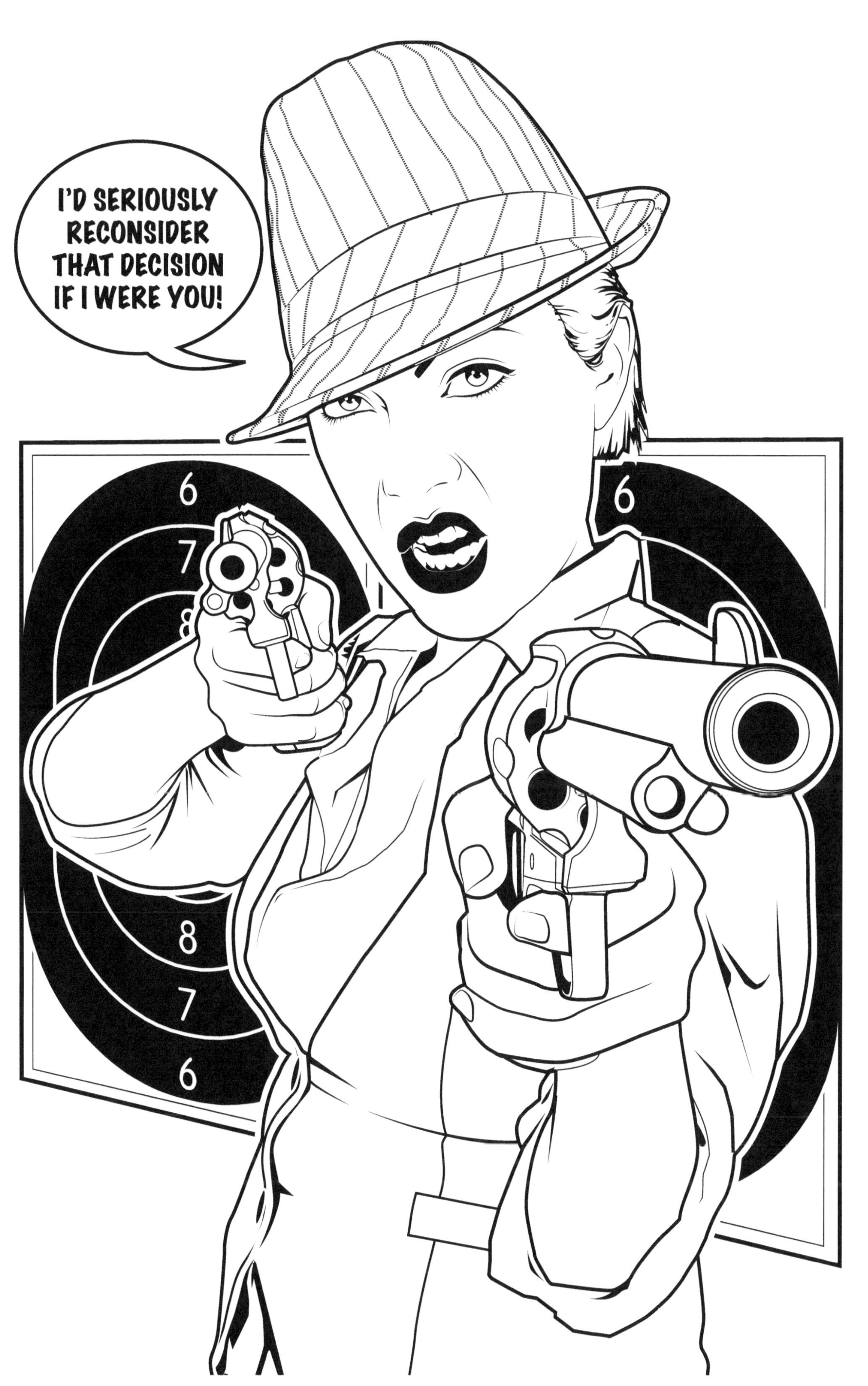
I'D SERIOUSLY RECONSIDER THAT DECISION IF I WERE YOU!
6
7
8
6
8
7
6

To be honest, there are better things
to do at night than fight crime.

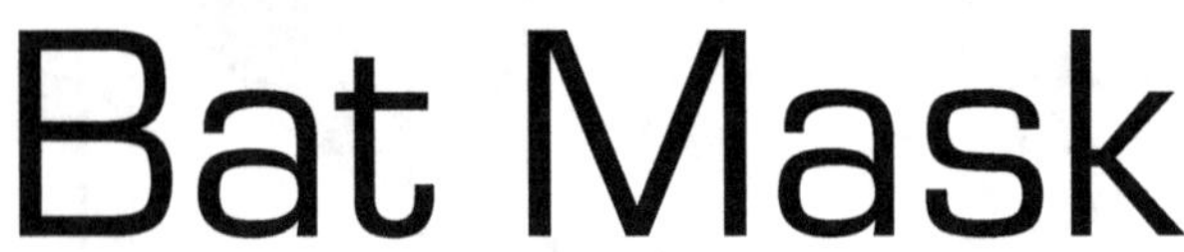

Bat Mask

Model: Libby Loo

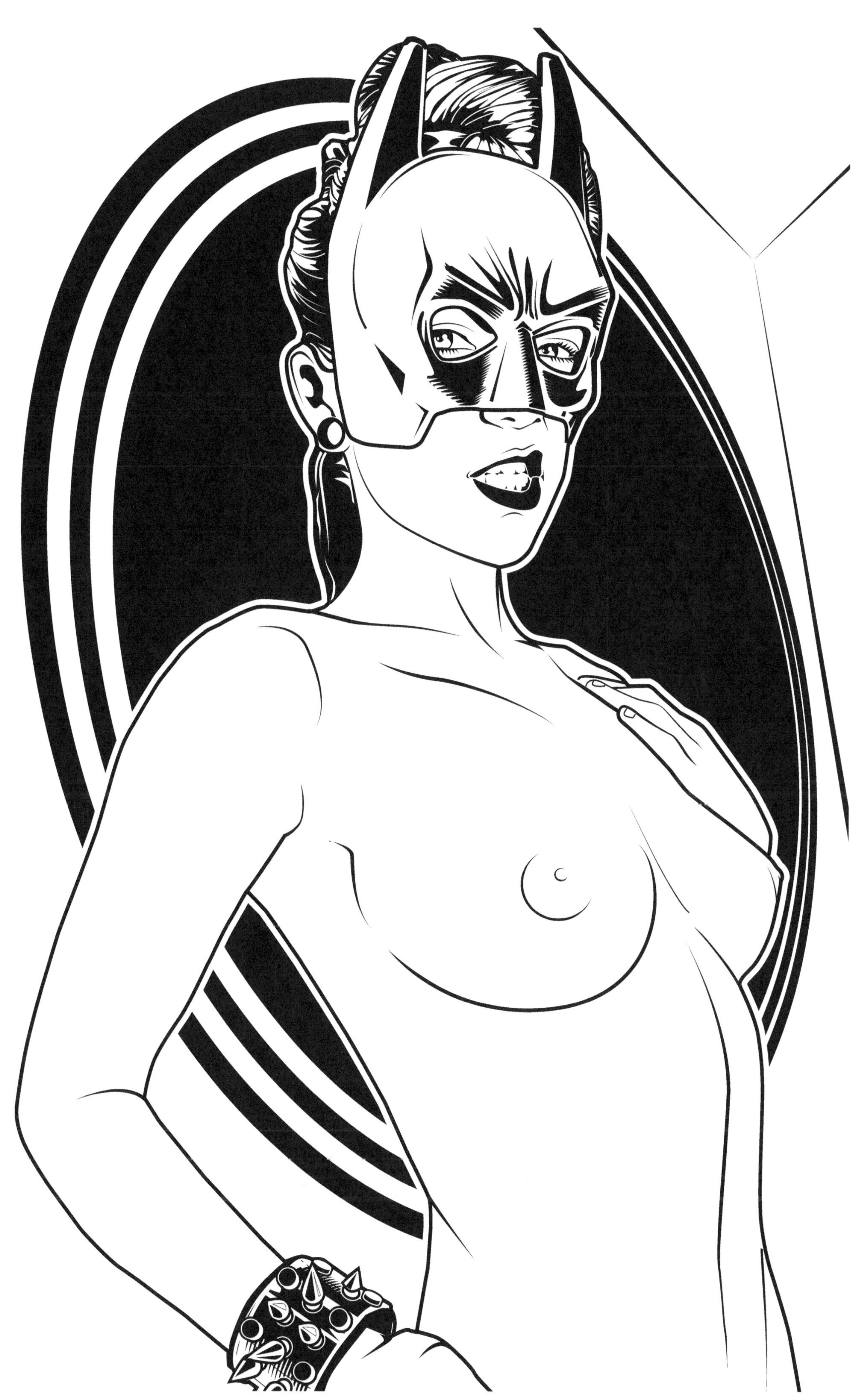

Are you sure you are ready for
this" she asked?

Personal Training

Model: Raven Le Faye

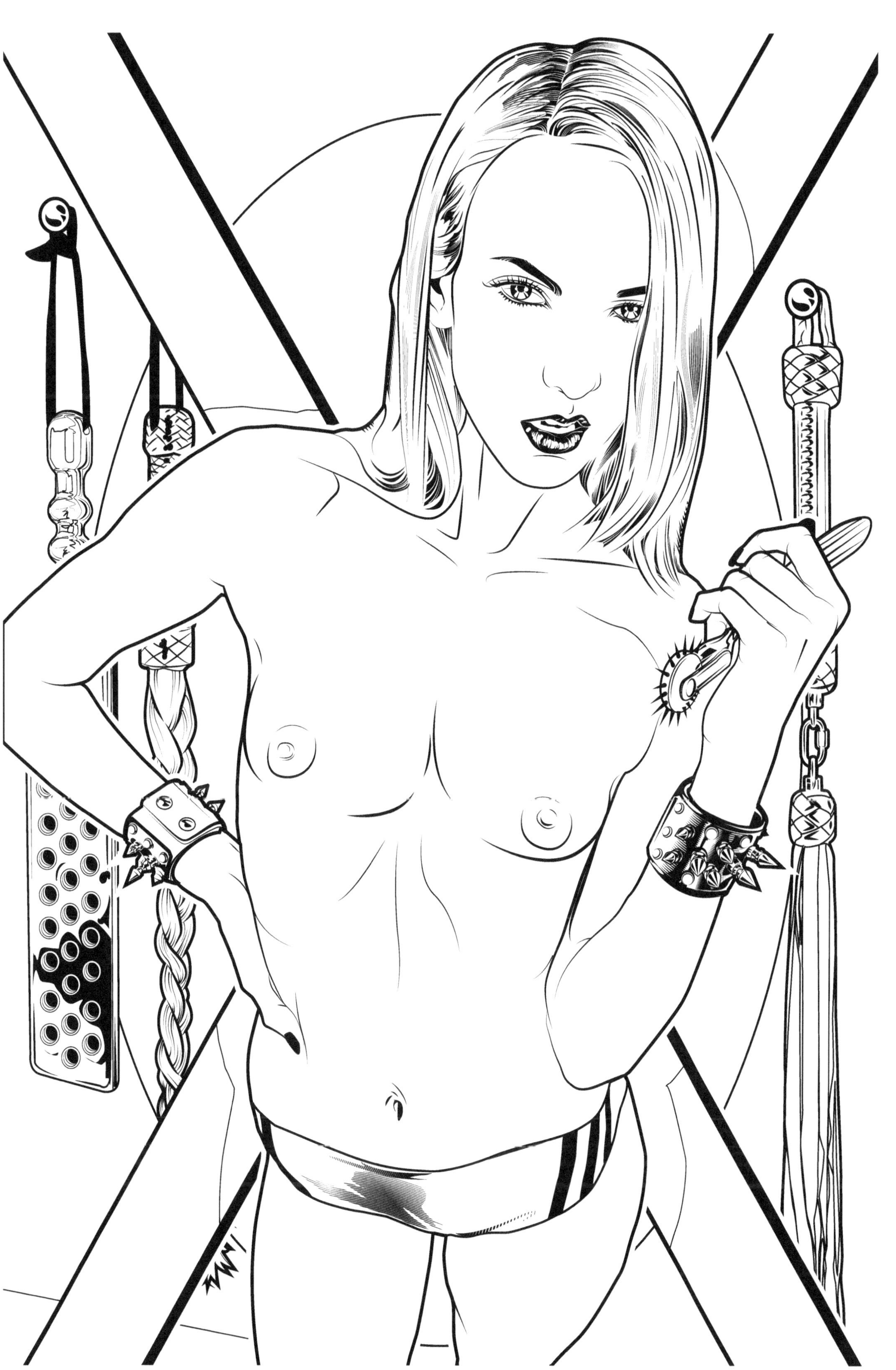

My Cousin Steve Ross's bike and the start of my love/hate relationship with drawing motorcycles.

Biker Booty

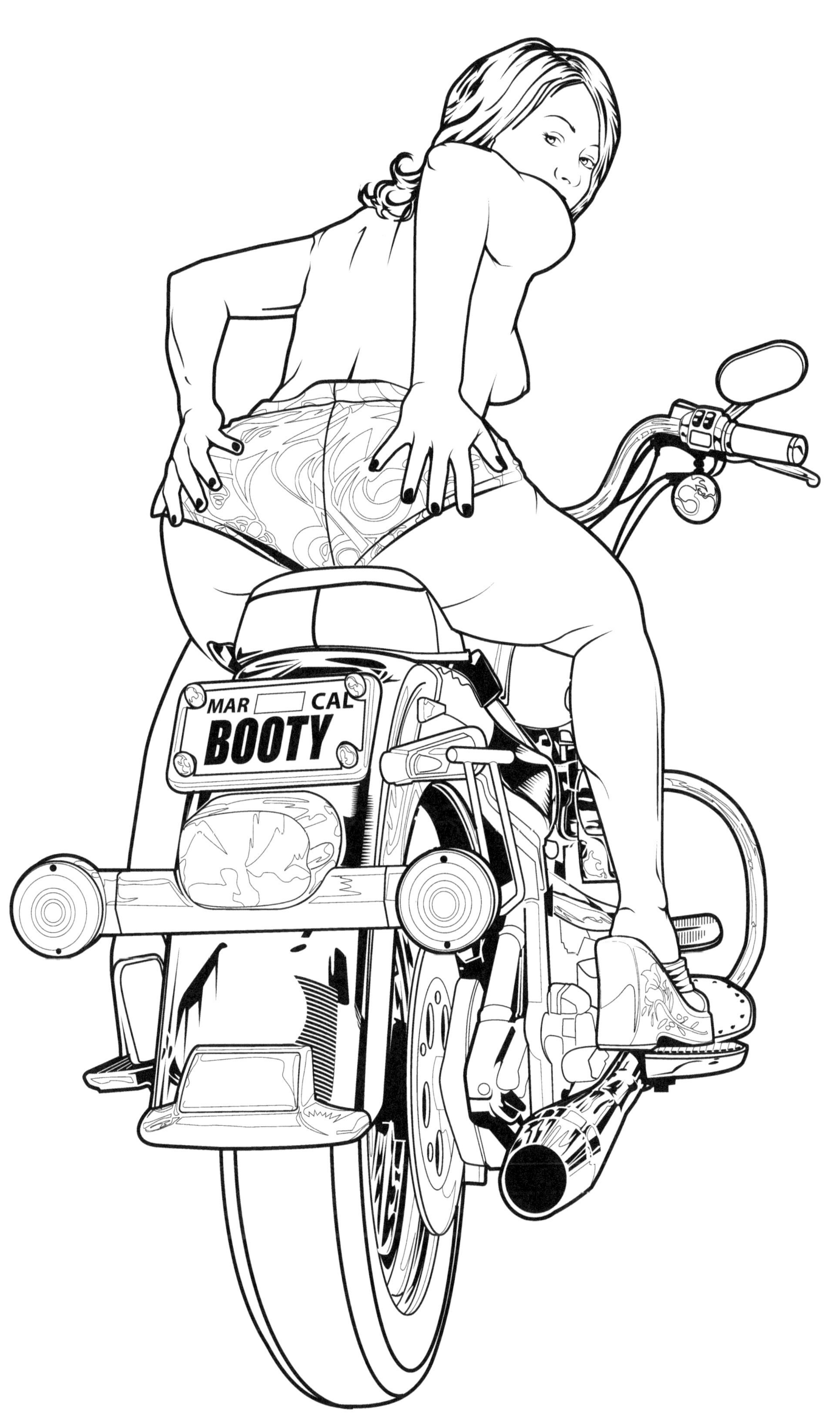
MAR CAL
BOOTY

When shooting HisDame, Corrupt-Morals brought out this solid metal collar he made and suggested it as something we could use to shoot with. It was big and heavy but her eyes would light up everytime the thing came out. I don't think that she would have forgiven me if I didn't shoot her in it.

Wearing His Collar

Model: HisDame

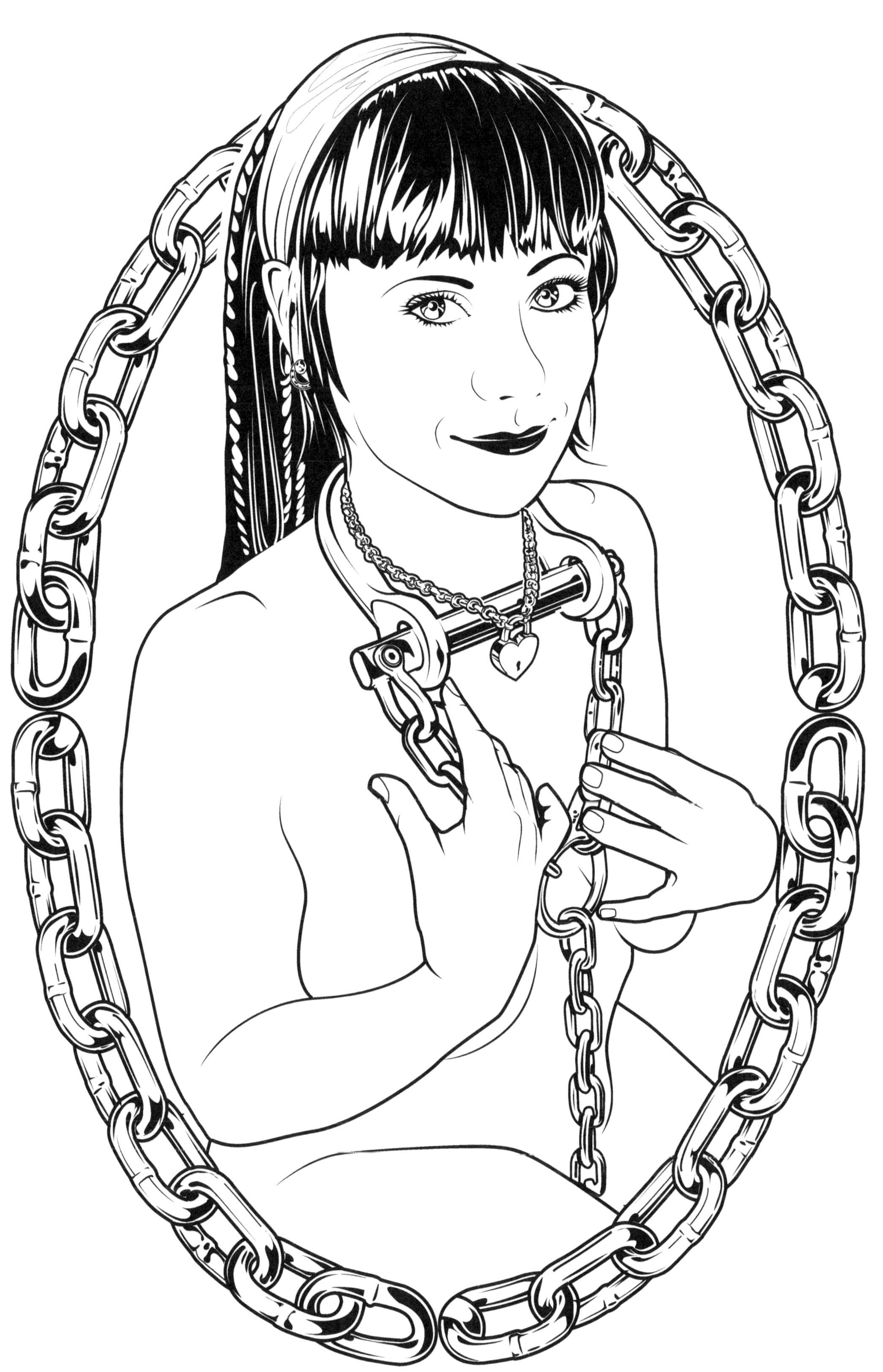

Though it has been a number of years since Mel and me lasted worked together, it seems that every year I have to do at least one illustration from that shoot. Sort of like a good luck piece.

Wanted Outlaw

Model: Melisande

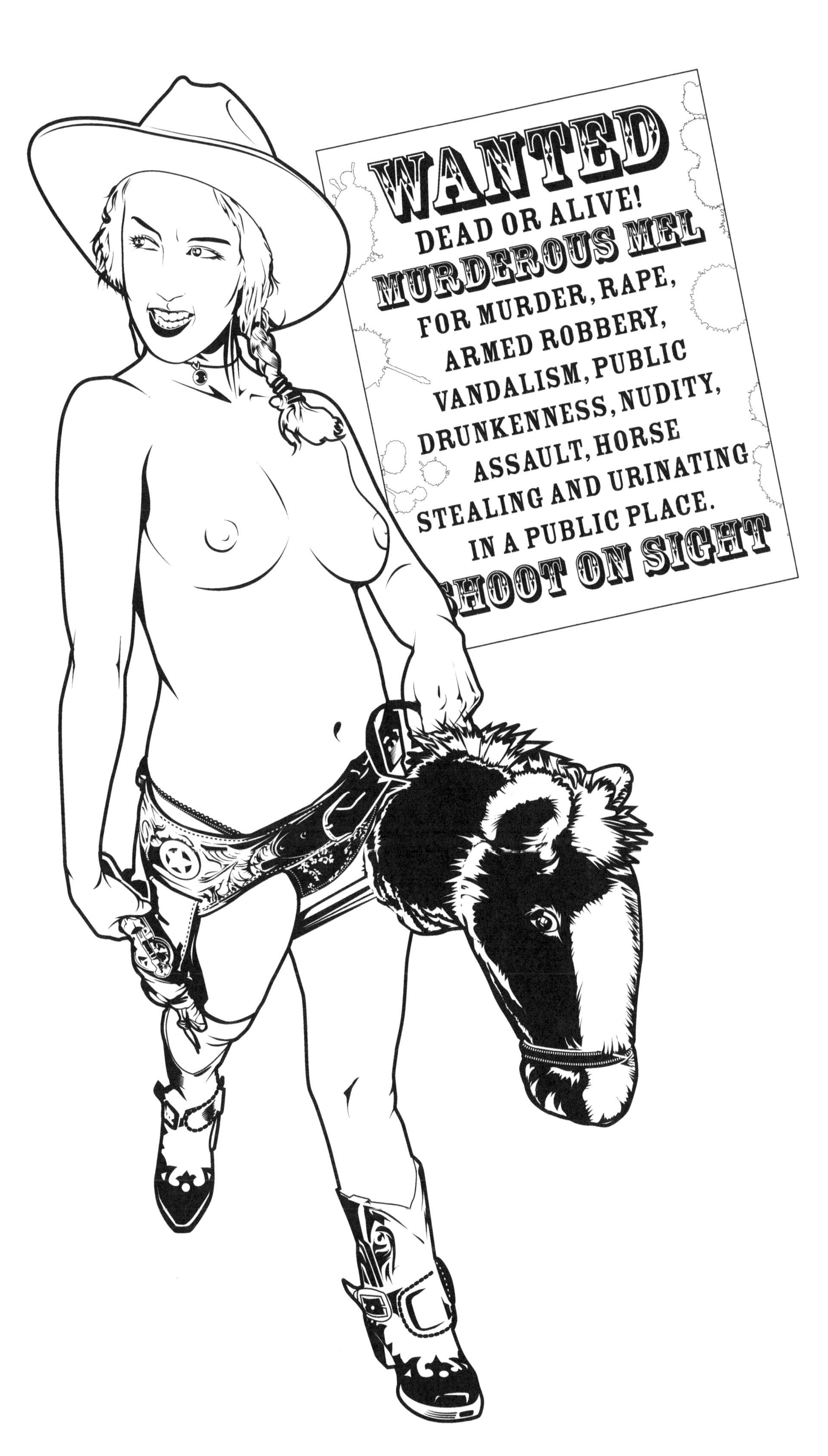
WANTED
DEAD OR ALIVE!
MURDEROUS MEL
FOR MURDER, RAPE,
ARMED ROBBERY,
VANDALISM, PUBLIC
DRUNKENNESS, NUDITY,
ASSAULT, HORSE
STEALING AND URINATING
IN A PUBLIC PLACE.
SHOOT ON SIGHT

Drawing Penny is always fun, but what I really liked making in this picture was creating the Queen Victoria Pasties.

Detective Penny

Model: Penny McClish

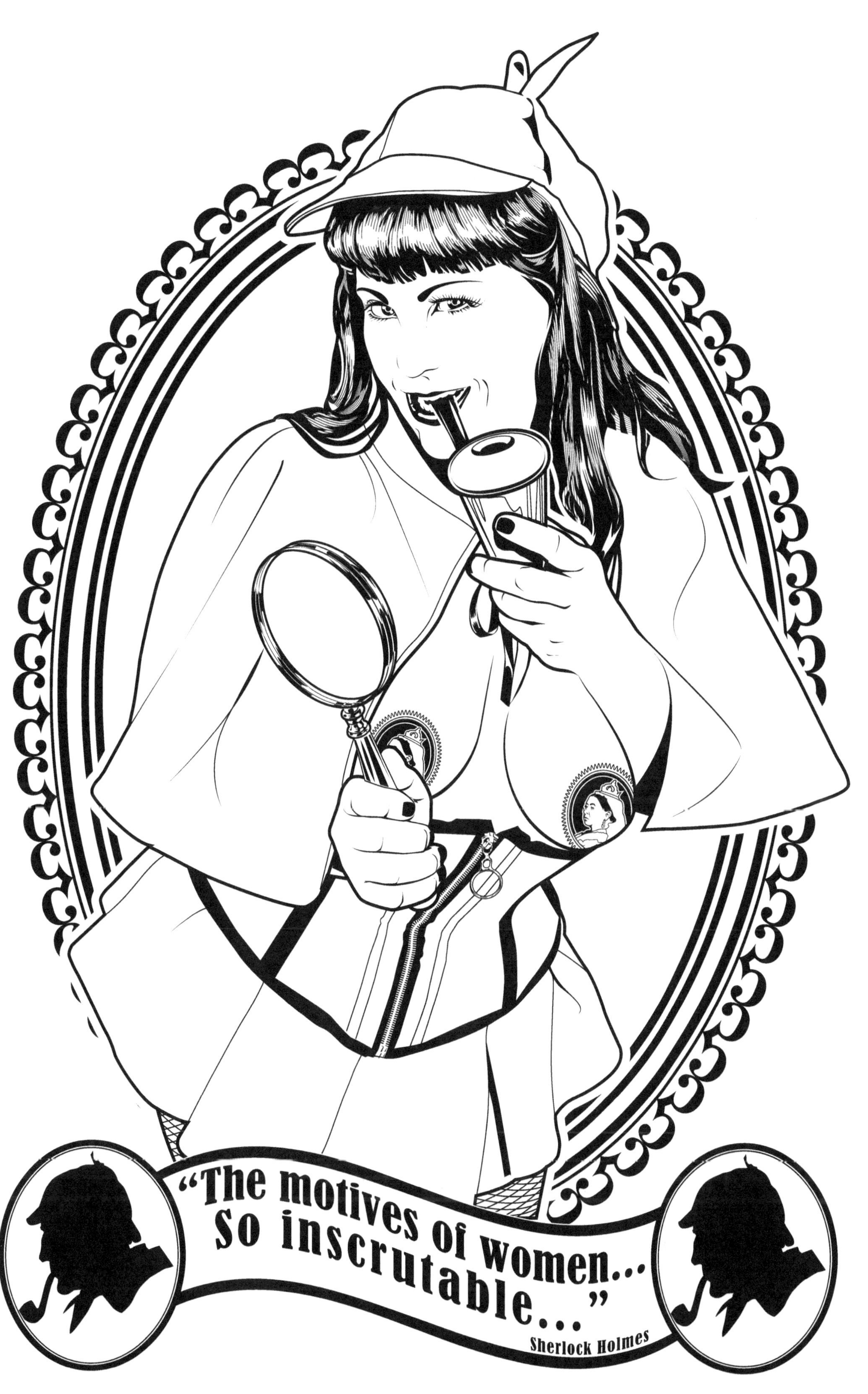
"The motives of women...
So inscrutable..."
Sherlock Holmes

Obviously, this one is not going on my Facebook page.

Flexible Kory

Model: Kory Vixen

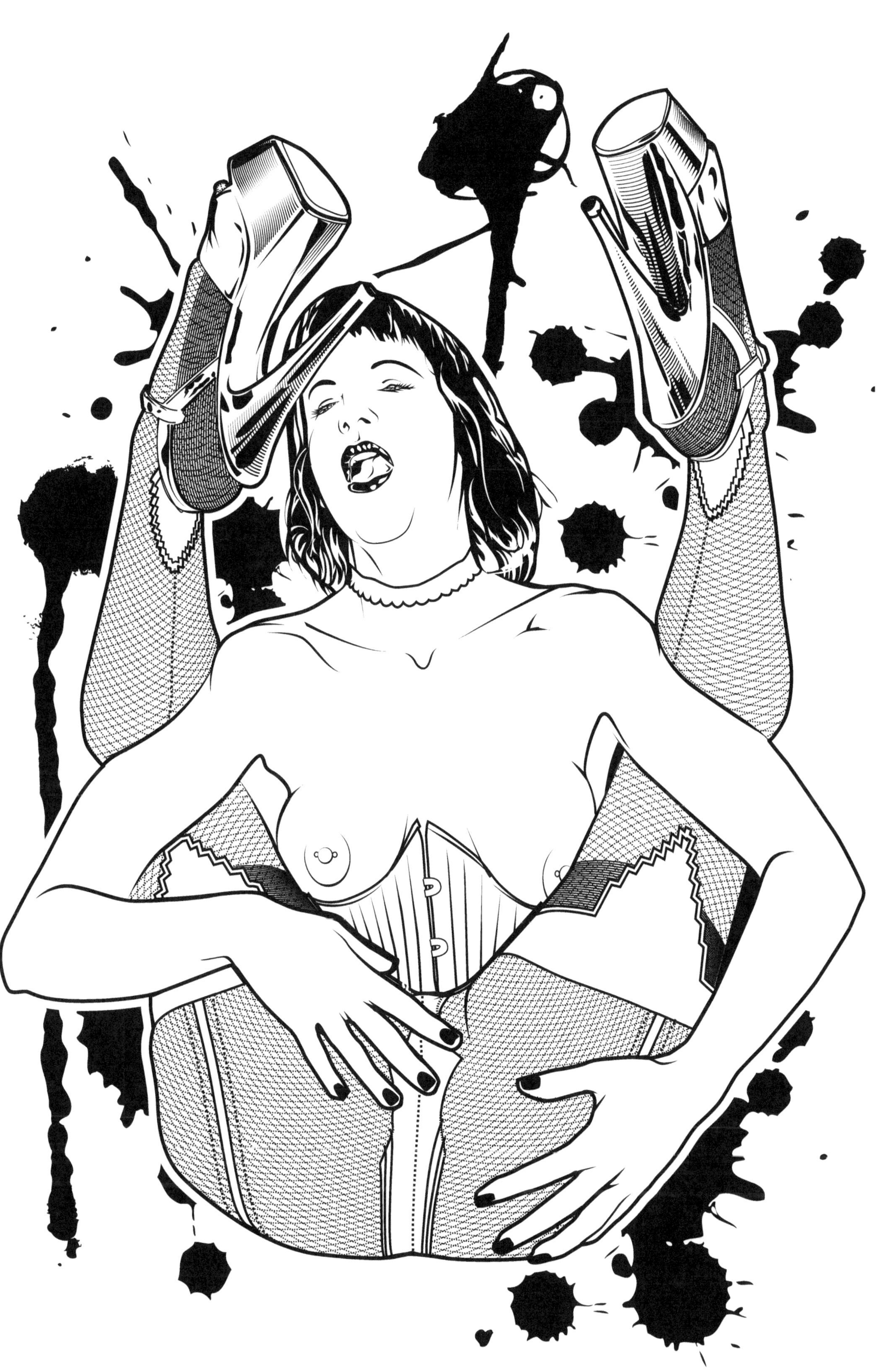

Remember, it is all about keeping Mistress happy.

Happy Mistress

Model: Stacey

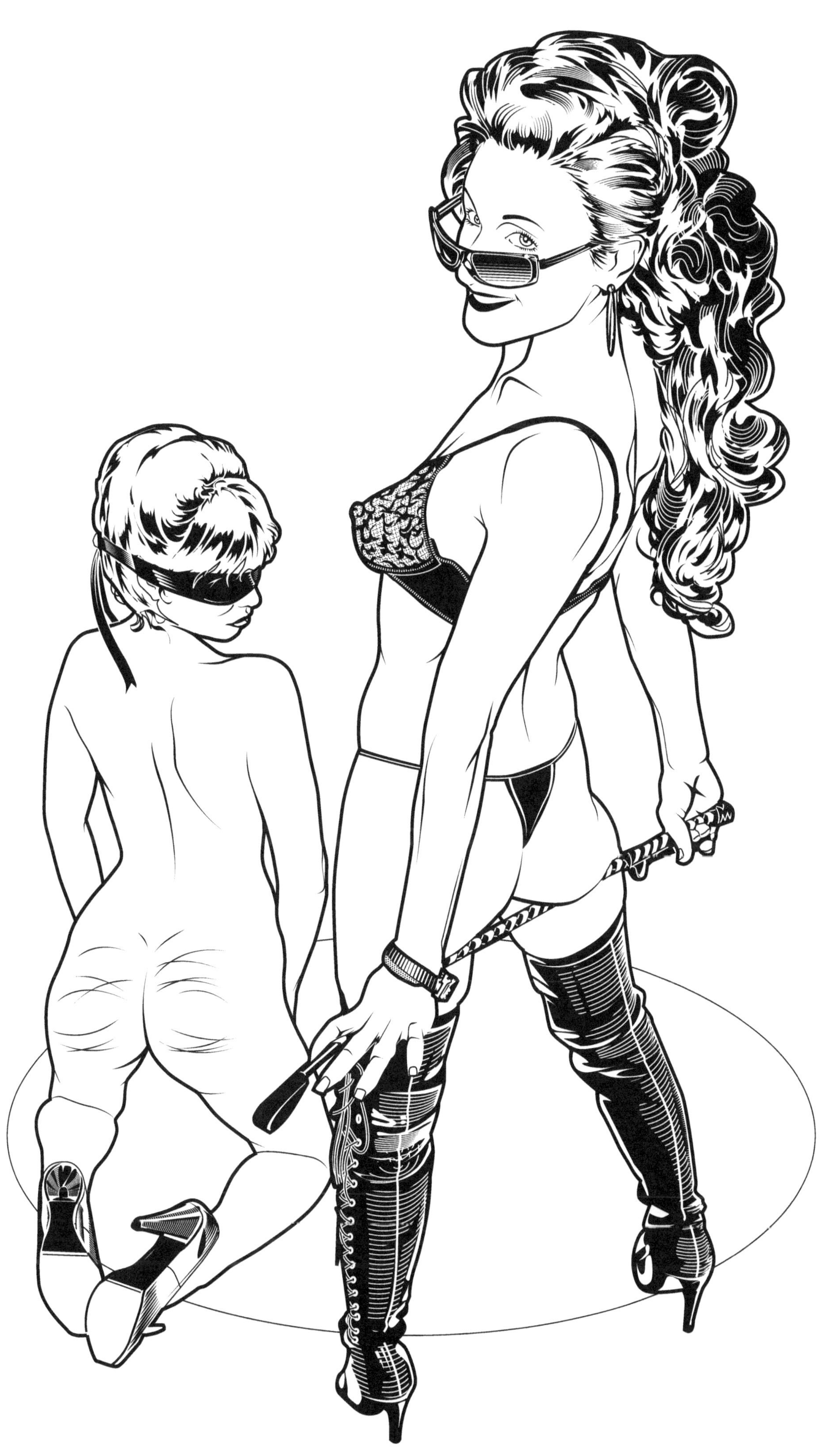

You'd think I would learn from past experiences about the difficulties in accurately trying to draw motorcycles. Hopefully Karina's headlights will blind anyone to any errors in my drawing.

Headlights

Model: Karina

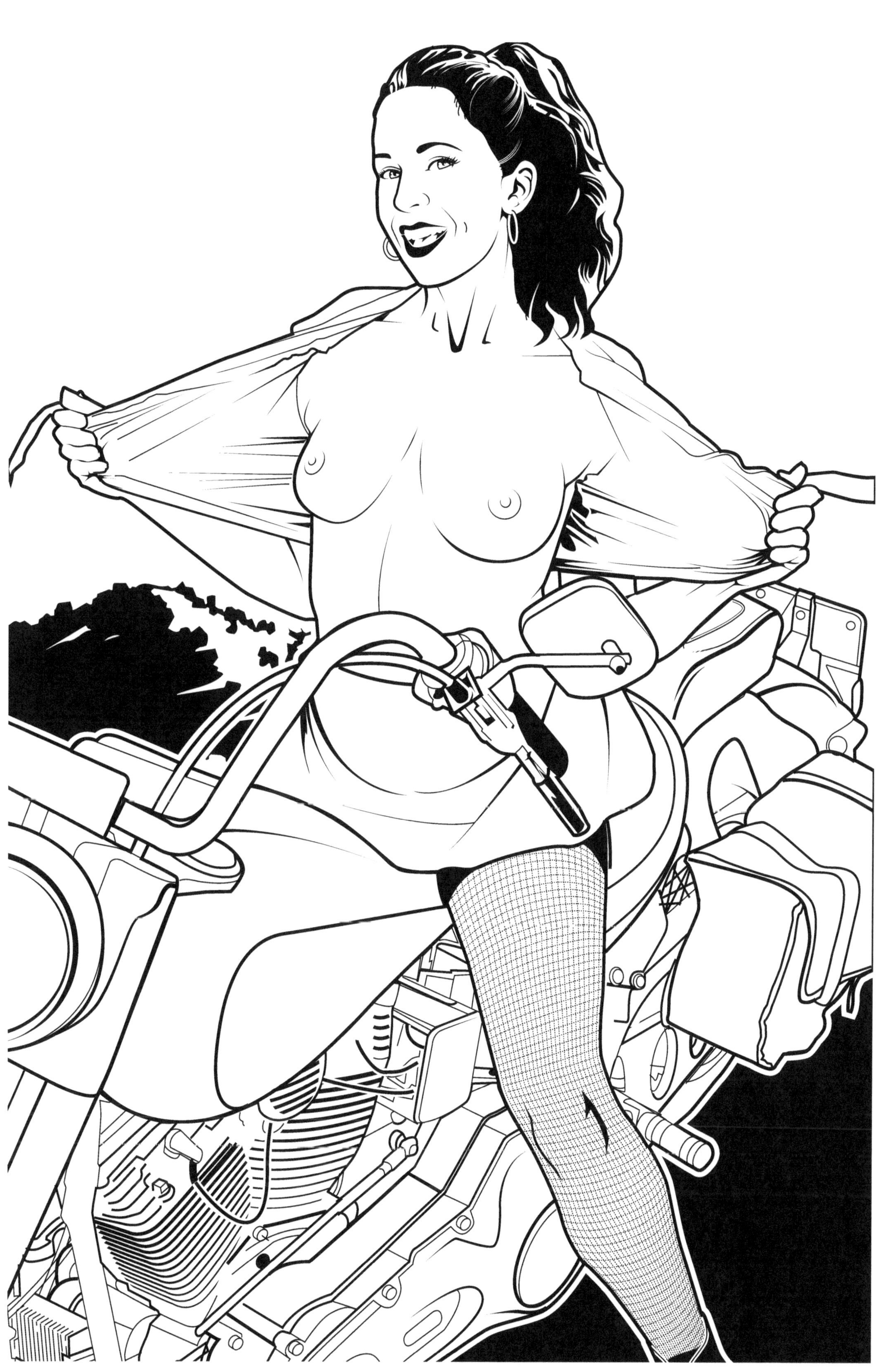

“Hand over your gold, silver and any lipstick or make-up supplies you may be carrying.”

Highway Woman

Model: HisDame

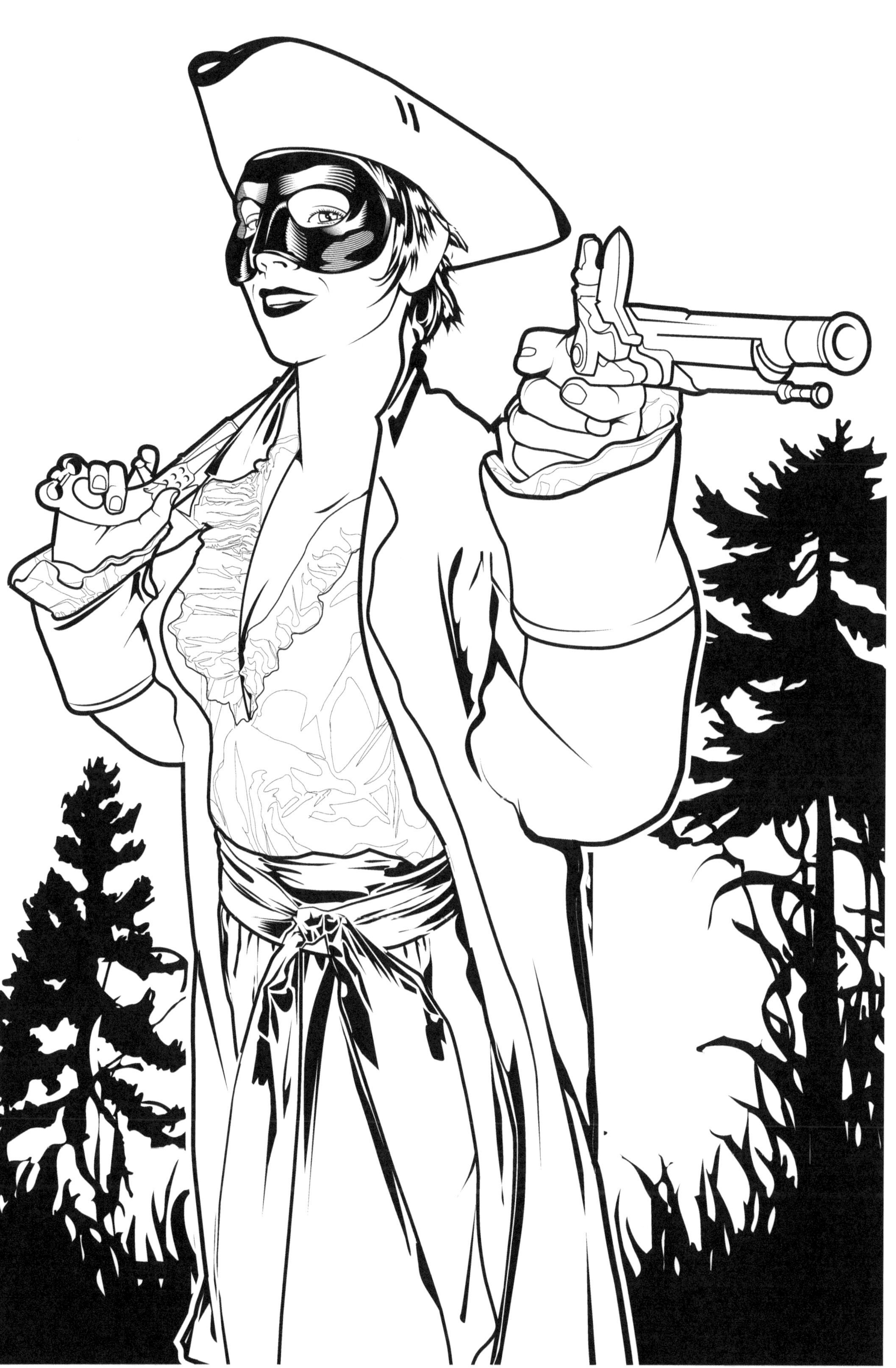

Anyone got a quarter?

Horsey Ride

Location: Folsom Street Fair, San Francisco

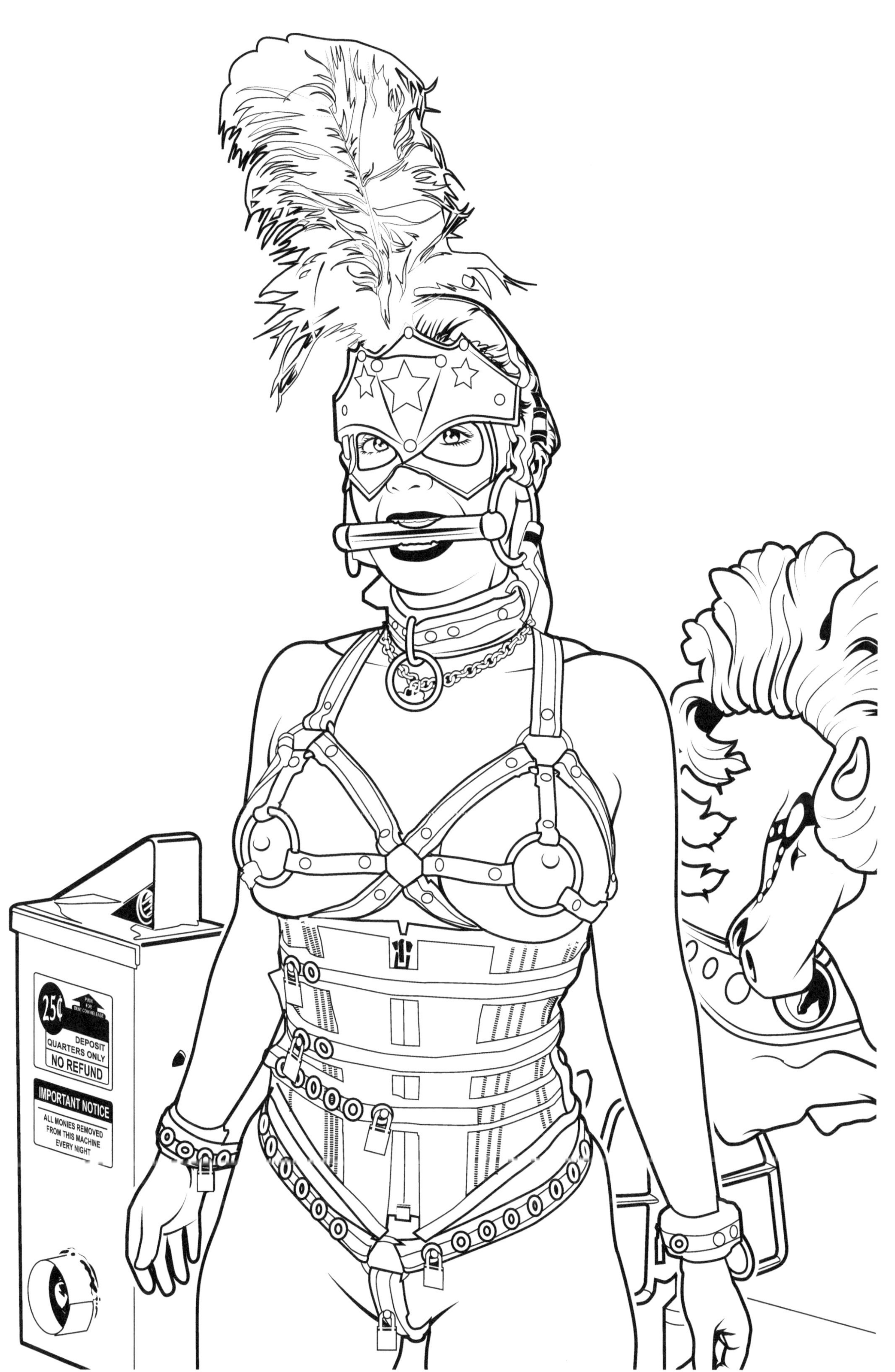
25¢
PUSH FOR BENT COIN RELEASE
DEPOSIT
QUARTERS ONLY
NO REFUND
IMPORTANT NOTICE
ALL MONIES REMOVED
FROM THIS MACHINE
EVERY NIGHT

For me, the sexiest women always
seem to be the most fearless.

Space Babe Bondage

Model: Cherry Katonic

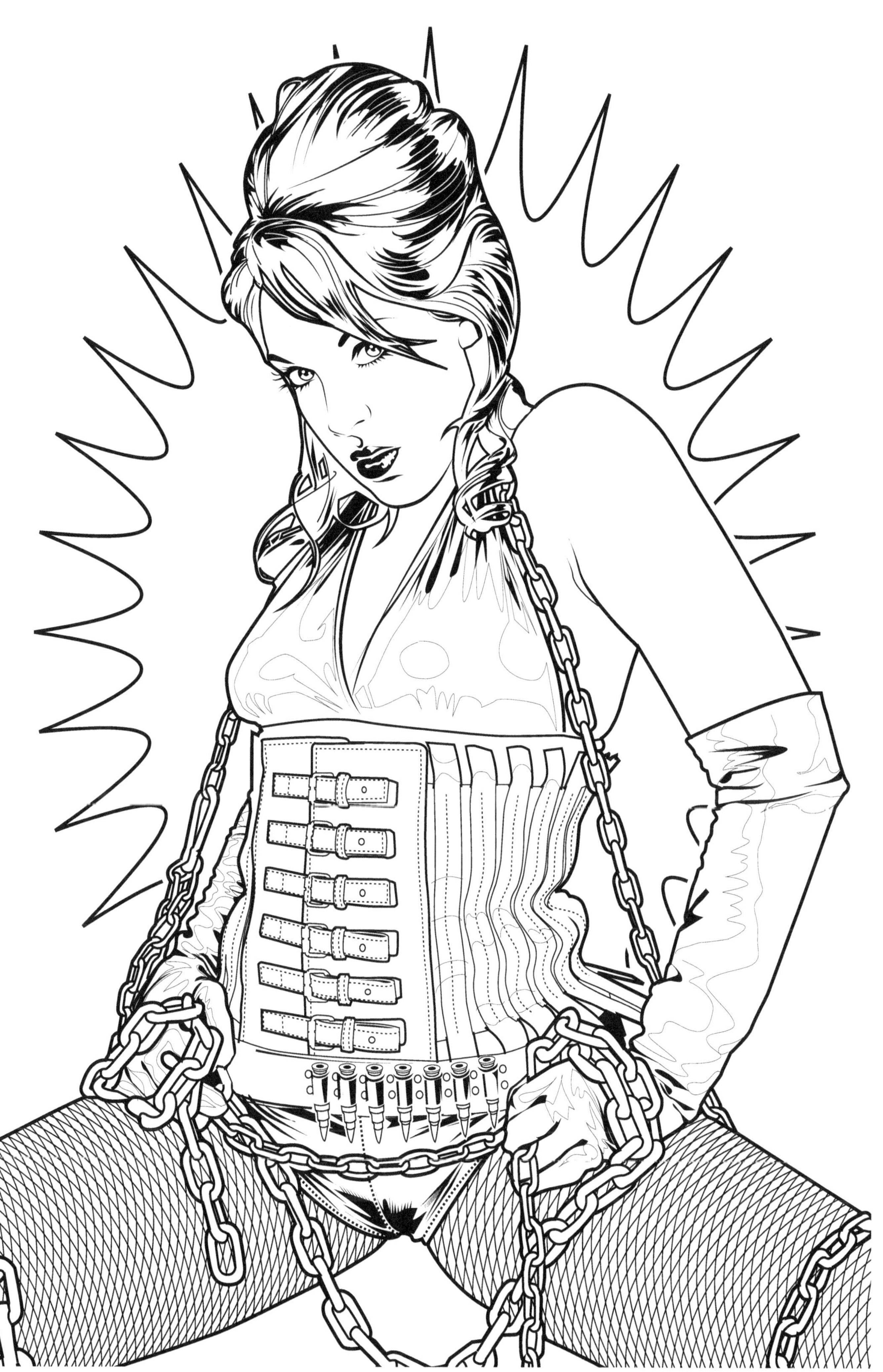

Some lessons can only be learned
the hard way.

Held After School

Models: Jesse Marie and Roxxie

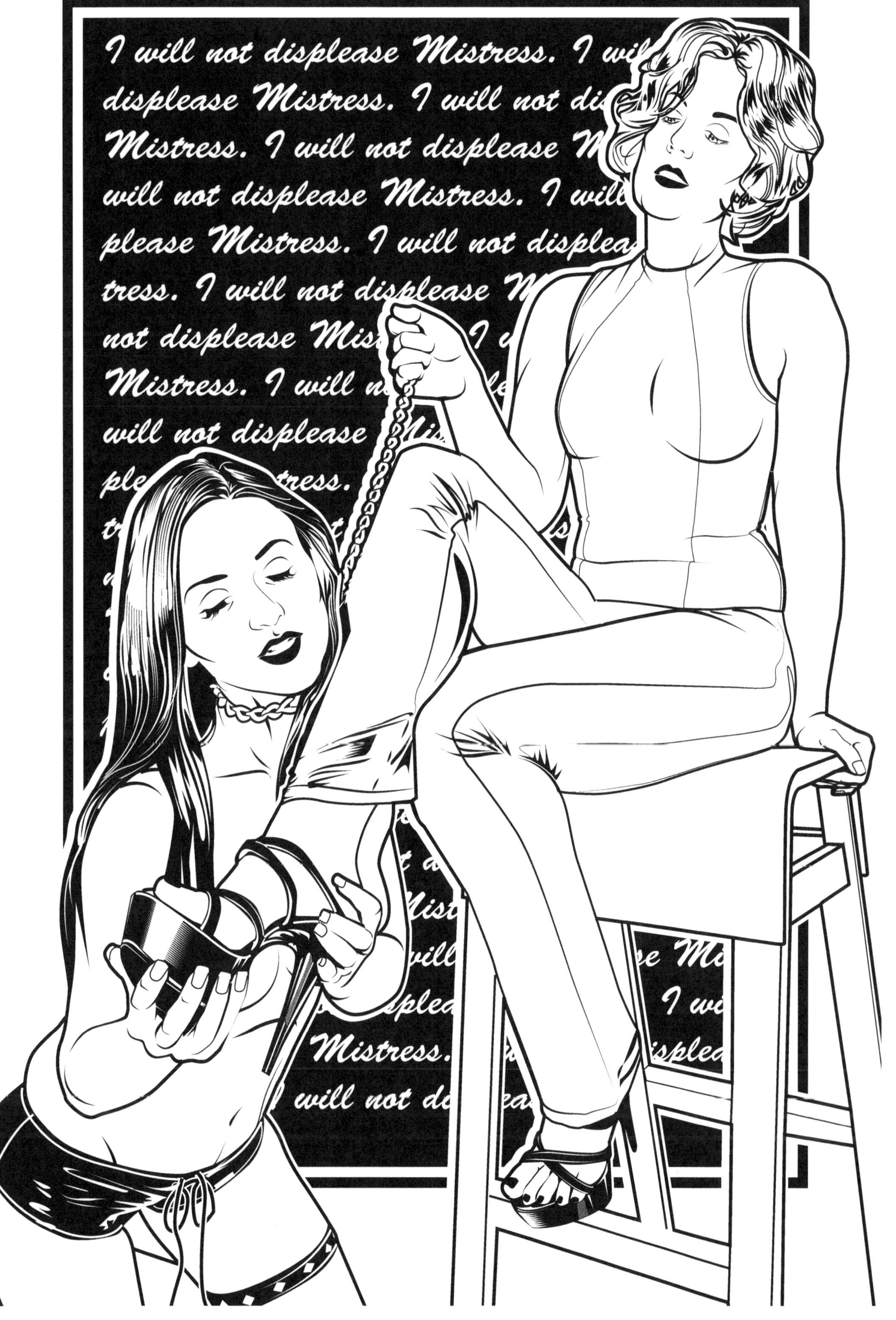
I will not displease Mistress. I
displease Mistress. I will not
Mistress. I will not displease
will not displease Mistress. I
please Mistress. I will not
tress. I will not displease
not displease
Mistress. I will
will not displease
tress.
Mistress.
will not

Deep down, we all like to watch.

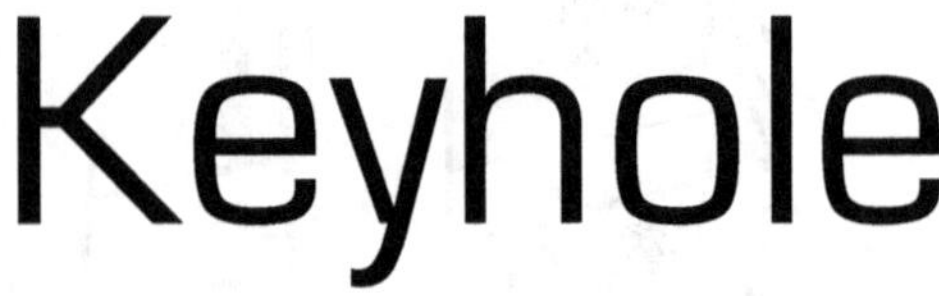

Model: Libby Loo

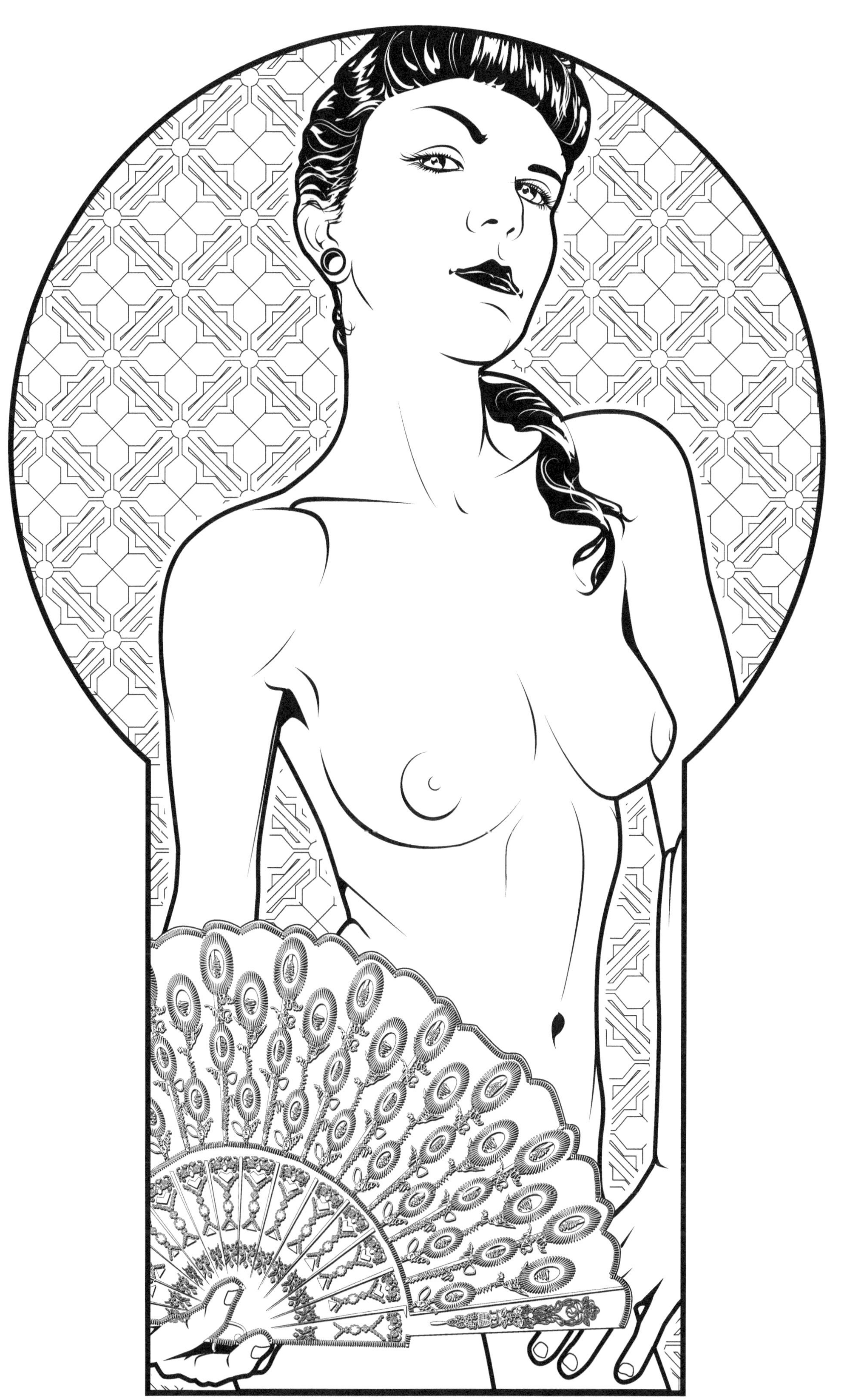

The sweetest, nicest person to
ever beat the crap out of you.

Mistress E.

Model: Elizabeth

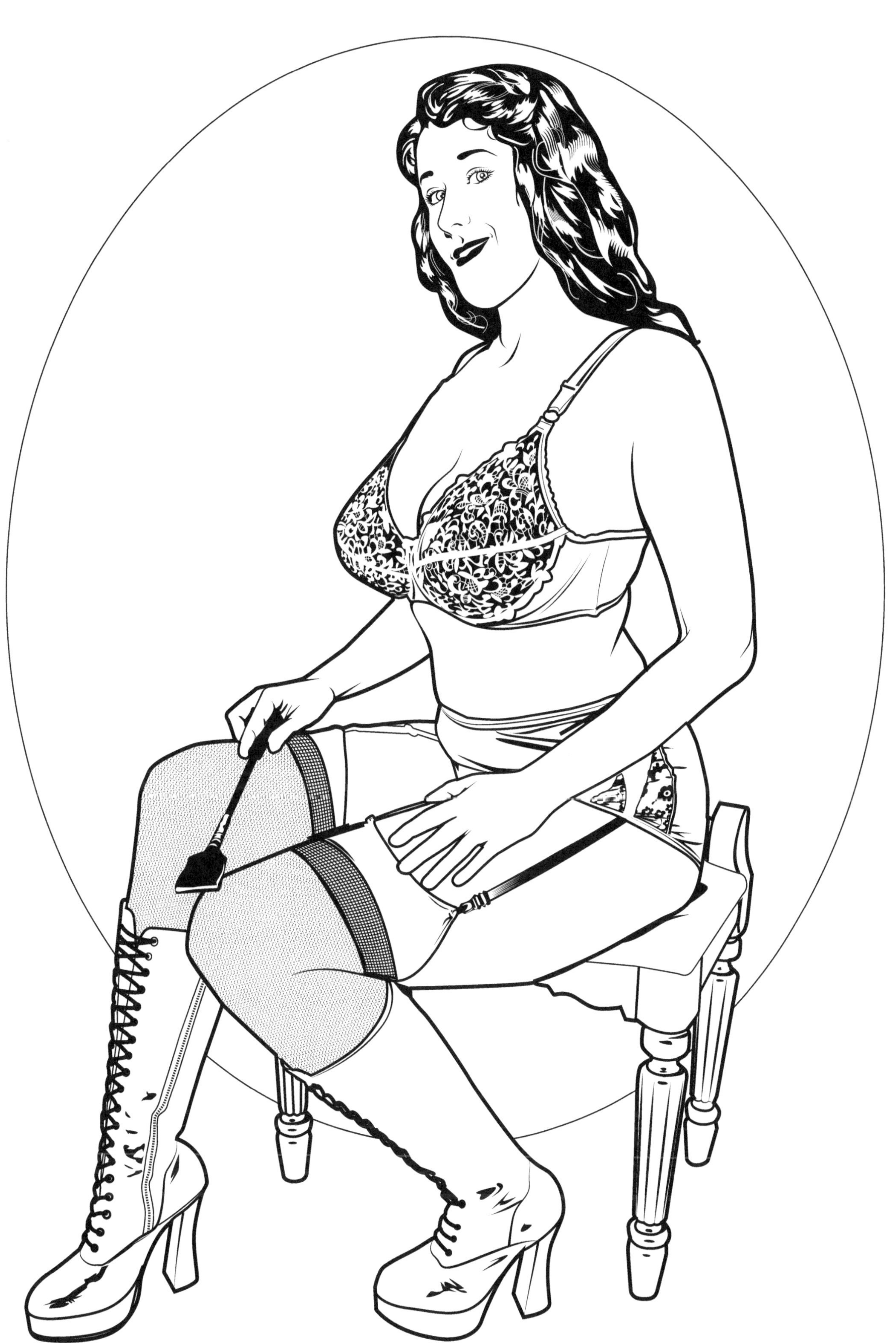

The irony of this picture, is that I felt I actually had to draw some more tattoos to Basia at the time. Seems Basia has felt that she needed more tattoos too and since added a lot. She is now the only model I work with that takes longer to draw naked than clothed. (But she is worth the effort.)

Nursing Basia

Model: Basia

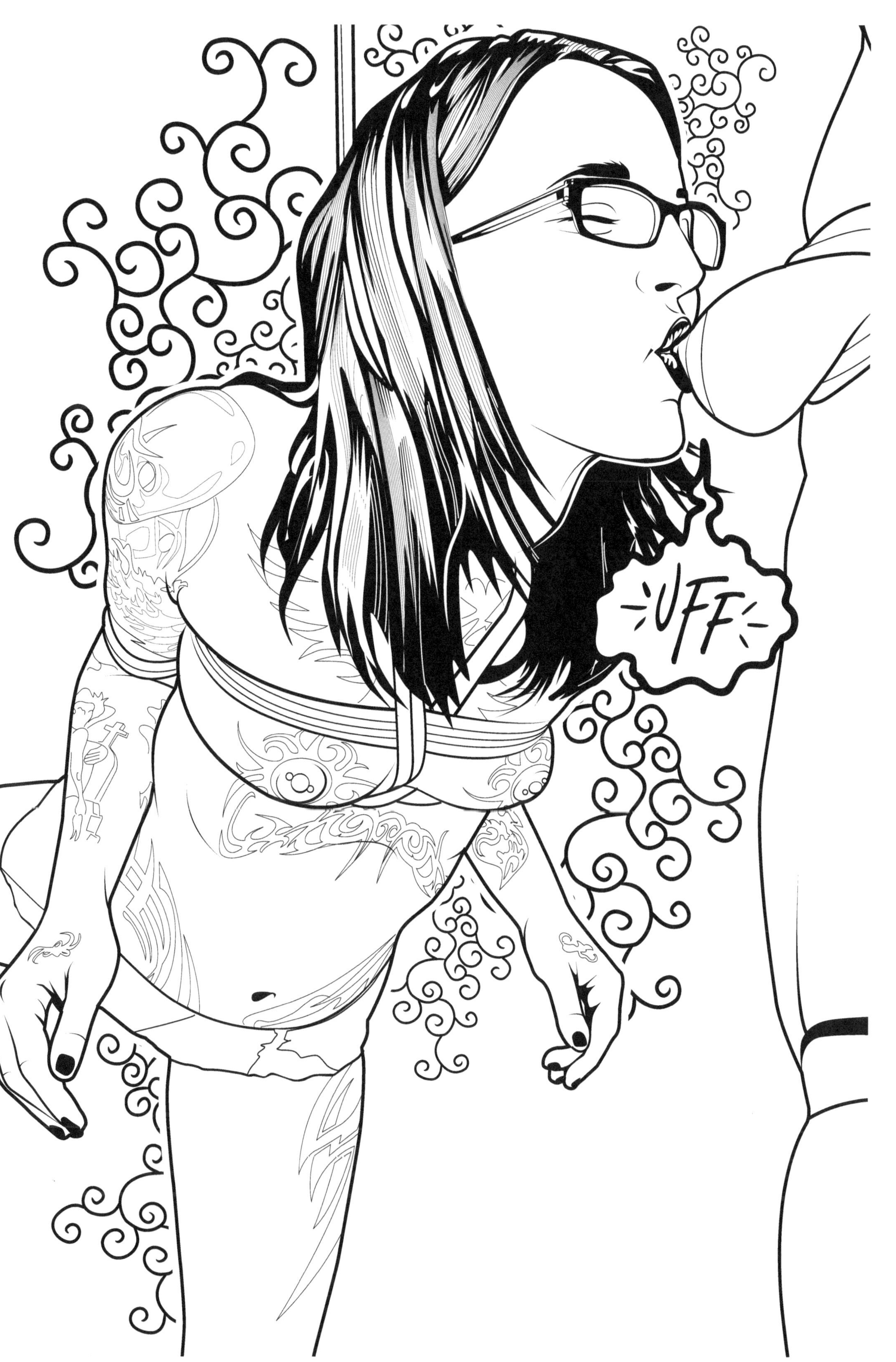
UFF

Drawing motorcycles and rope is sort like hitting yourself in the head with a hammer. It usually feels the best when you finally stop.

Motorcycle Bondage

Model: Raven Le Faye

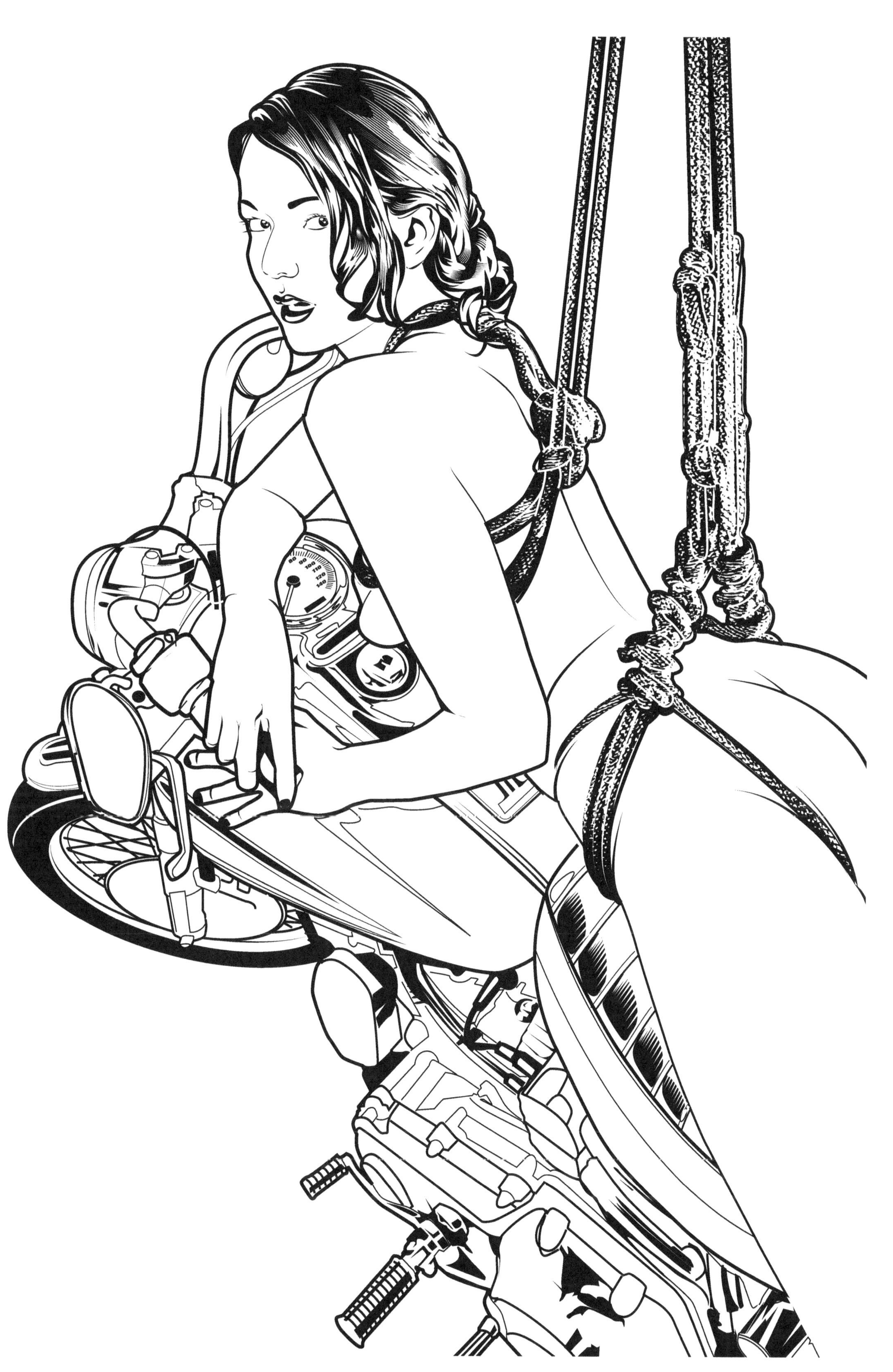

This piece was a lesson not to give up so easily. I had a lot of problems with it's design in the beginning. At one point I had even put is aside into the "To Be Done Later" folder. The next day though I took it out and continued working on it. I'm happy with how it came out but was so glad when it was finished.

A Pretty Devil

Model: Scarlet Faux

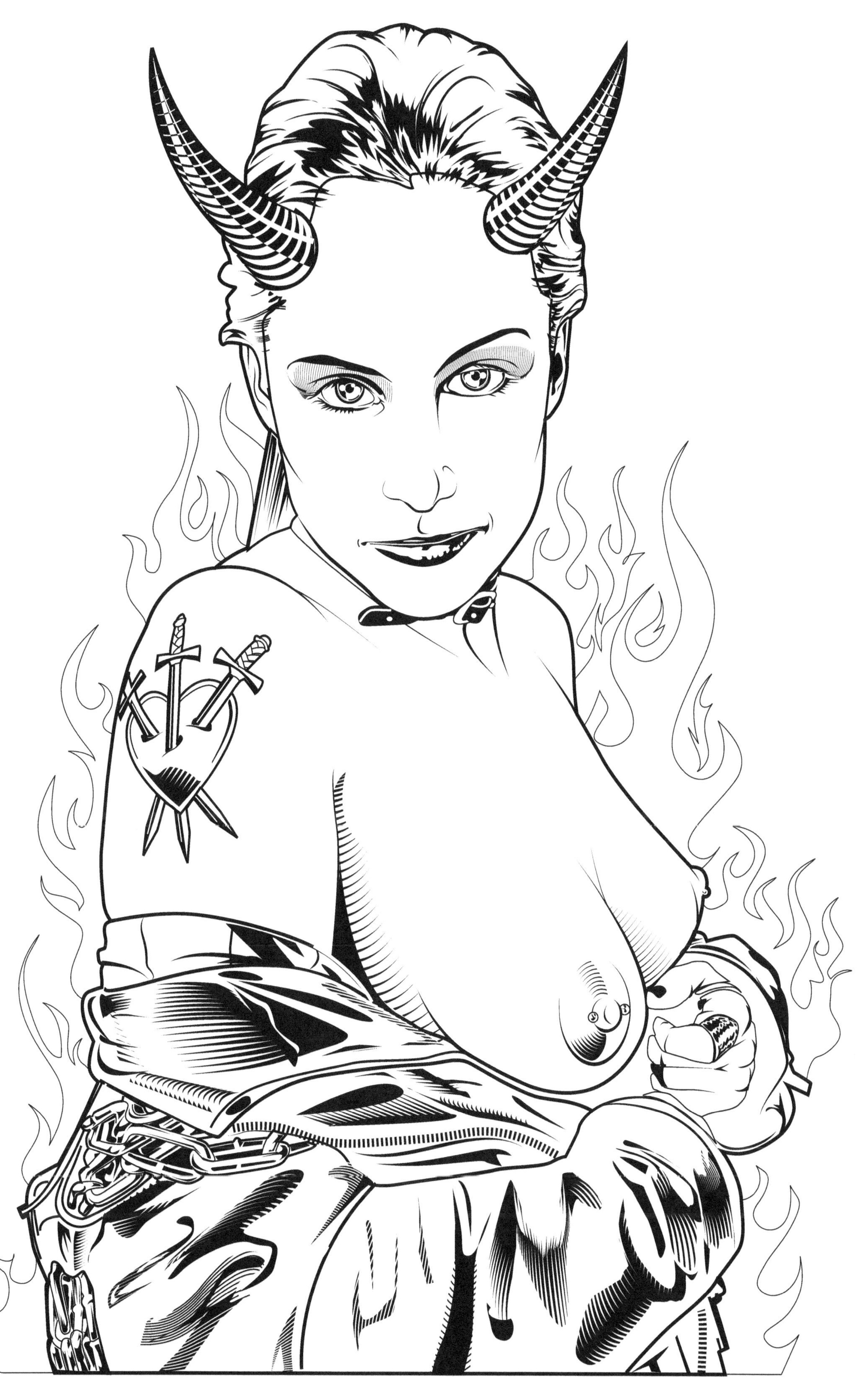

We have now moved on to electrical play.
I hope your PG&E bill is paid up.

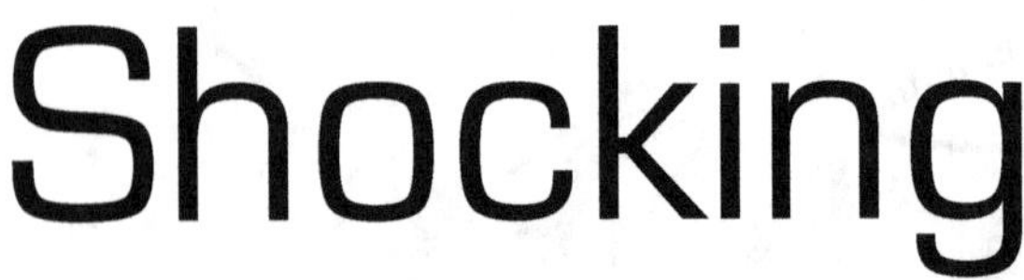

Models: Ned and Maggie Mayhem

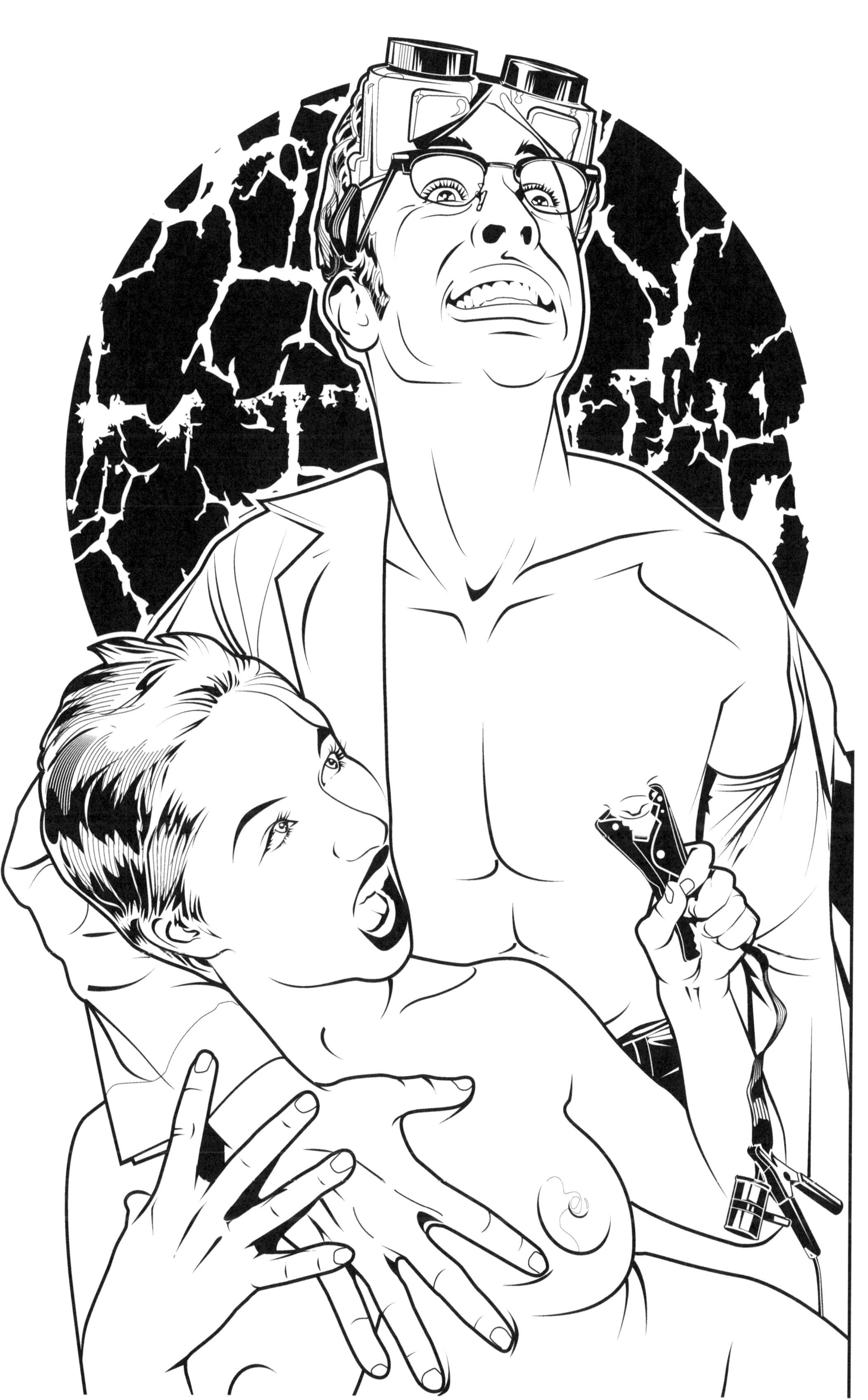

Built to perfection.

The 13th Cylon Model

Model: Chelsea Christian

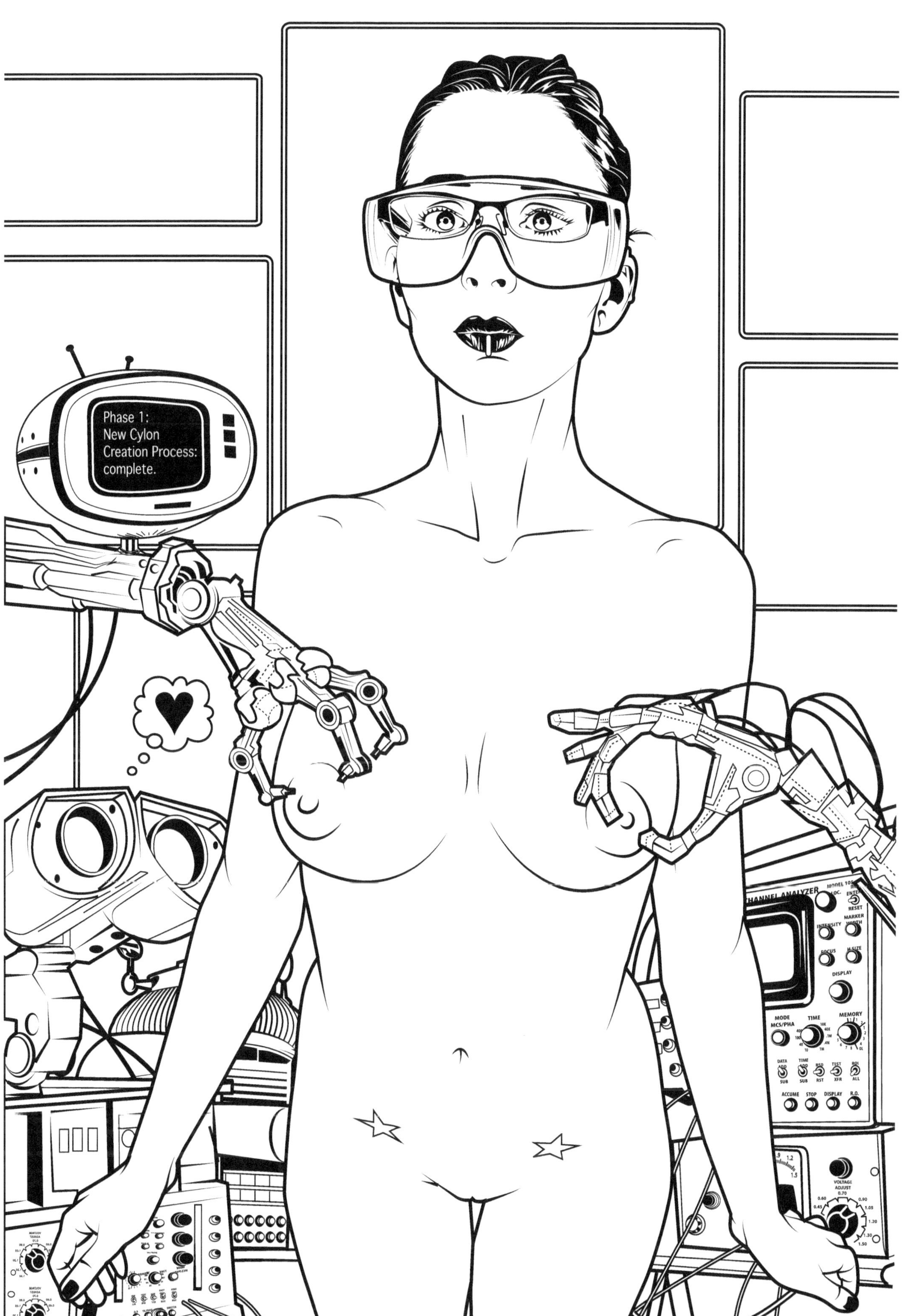
Phase 1:
New Cylon
Creation Process:
complete.

Cherry was such a fun and goofy model to work with, that it is almost surprising to me when I remember what a statuesque beauty she could also be.

Statuesque

Model: Cherry Katonic

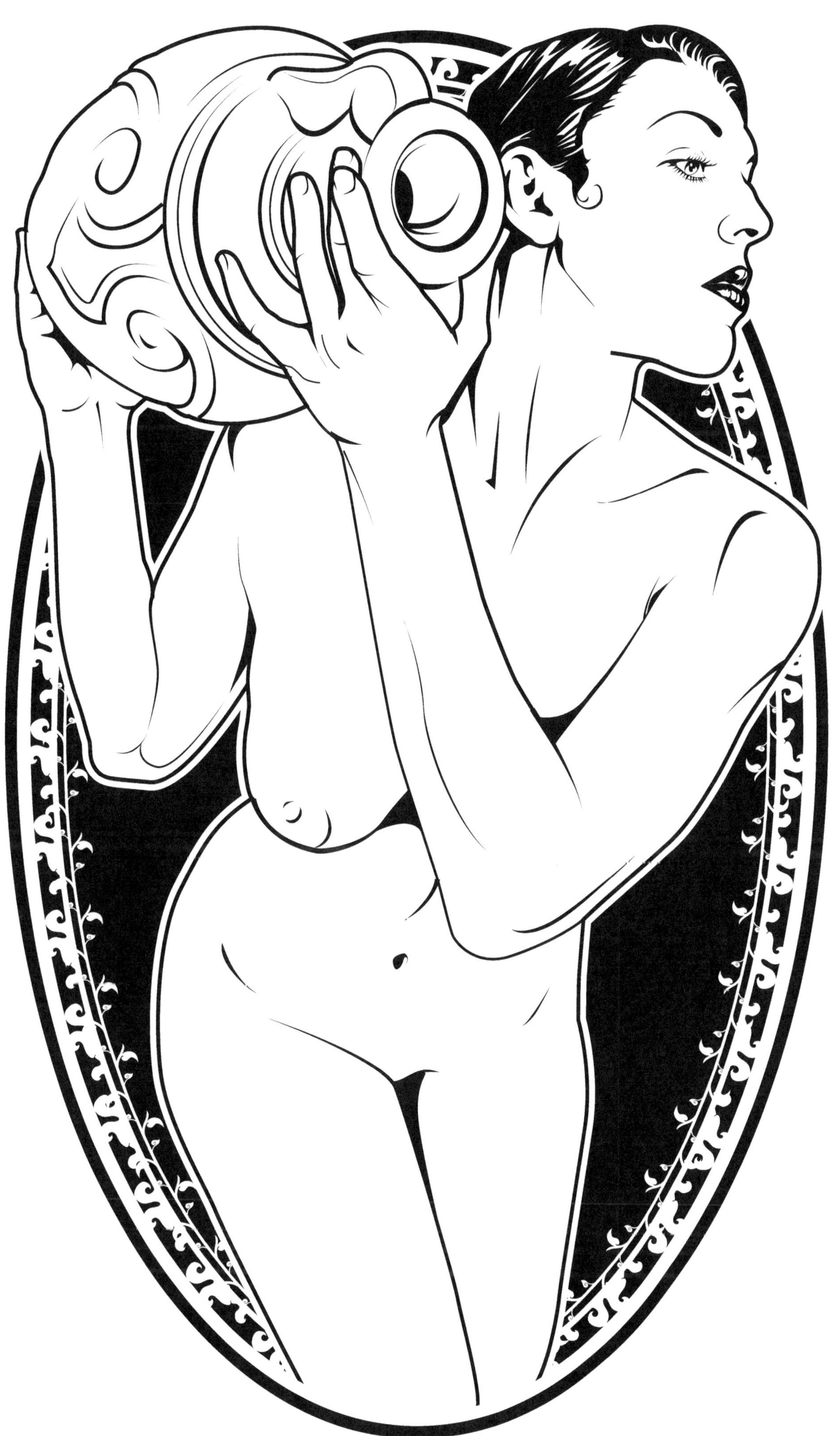

EnderSilence was a model I met at Michael Rosen's booth at the Folsom Street Fair in 2011. Later, I got a picture of her in front of another booth wearing this cool gas mask. She is definitely on my short list of models I want to work in the studio in the future. I mean, if she can look this good just standing around on the street...

Gasmask

Model: EnderSilence

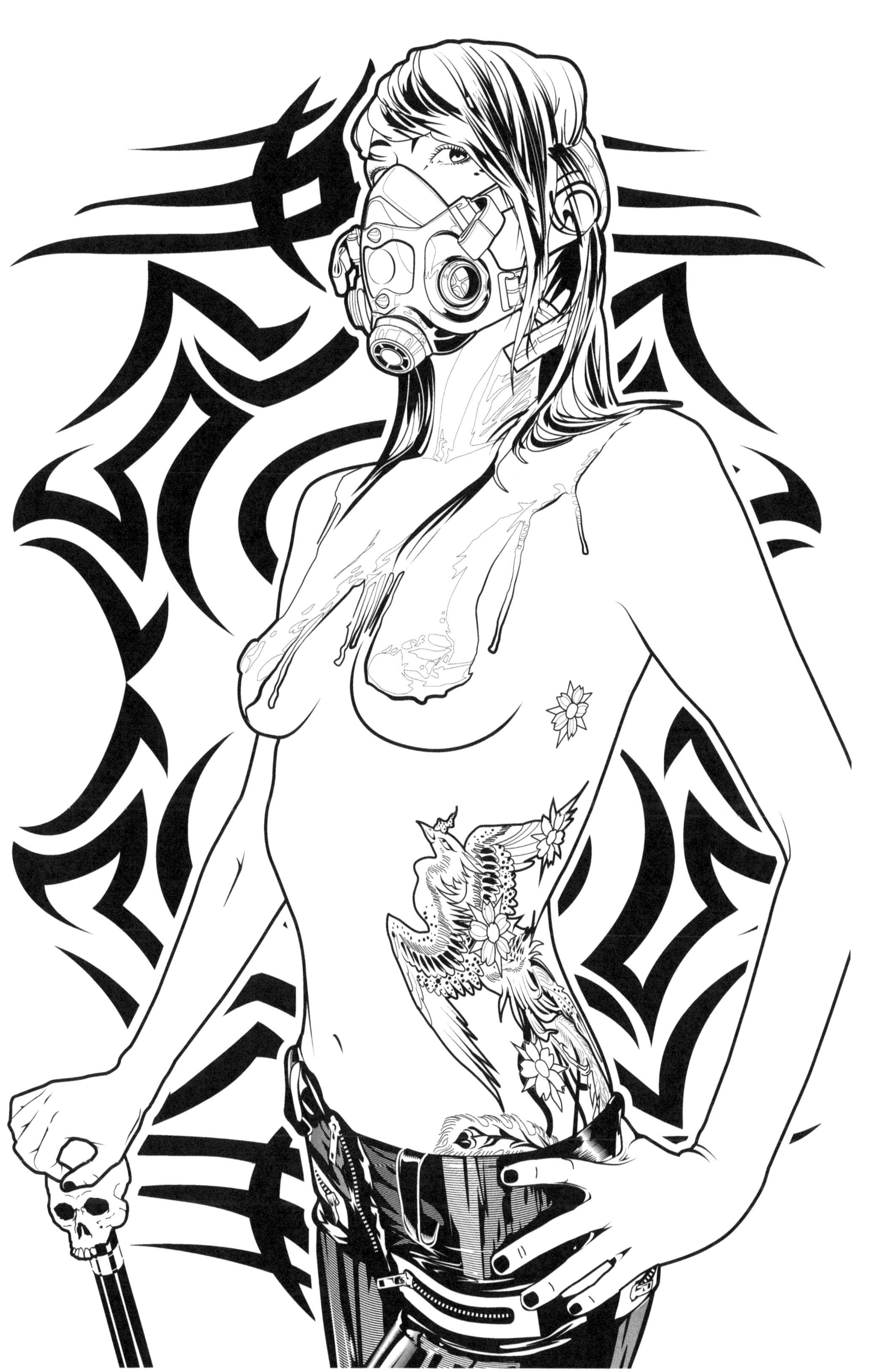

I posted a copy online of this image the day after Xmas 2011. Granted, this would be a better image for Halloween, but I didn't feel like waiting for nearly an entire year to share it.

Zombie Raven

Model: Raven Le Faye

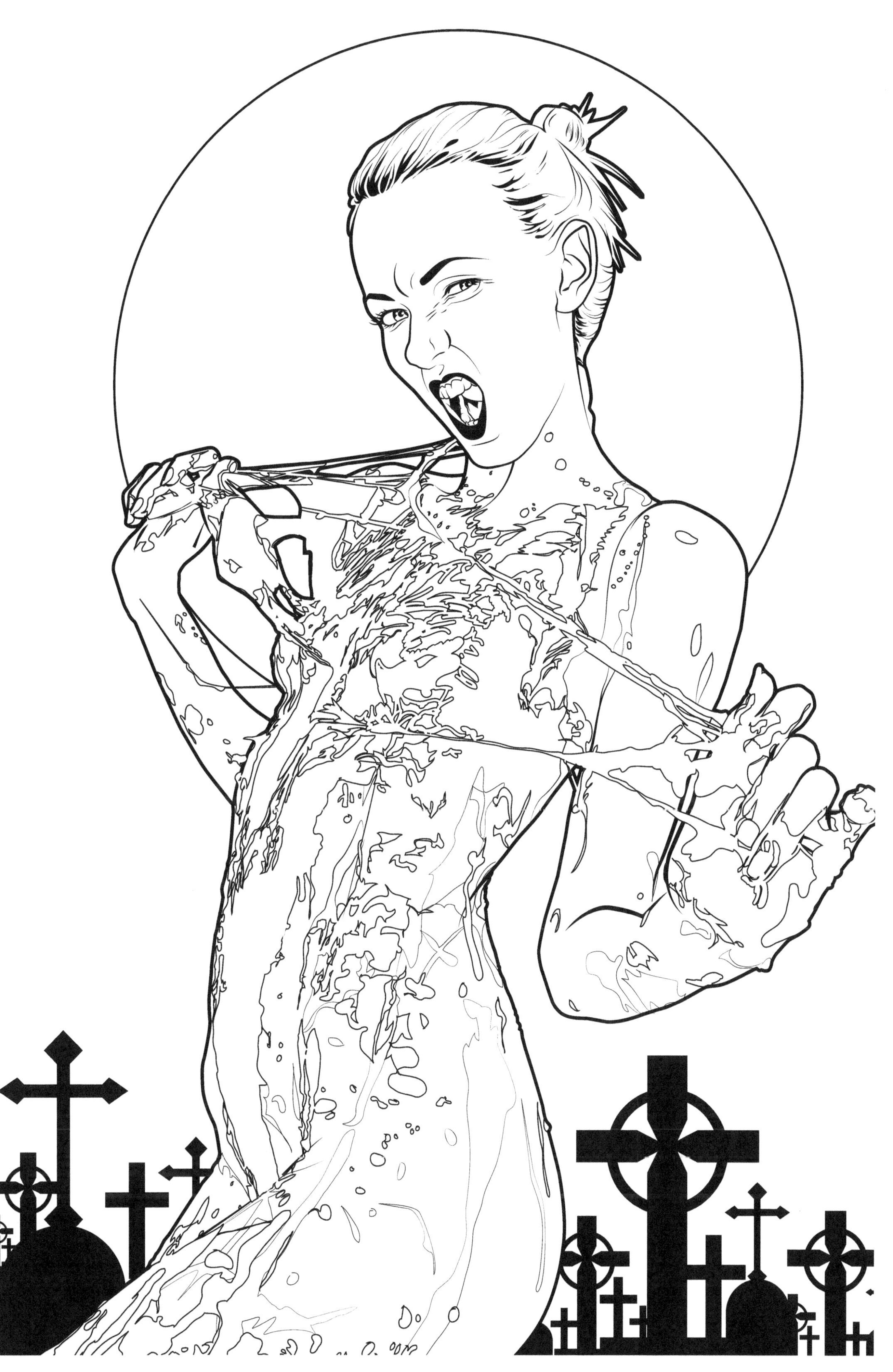

“I’ve Got The Power”

Model: Chelsea Christian

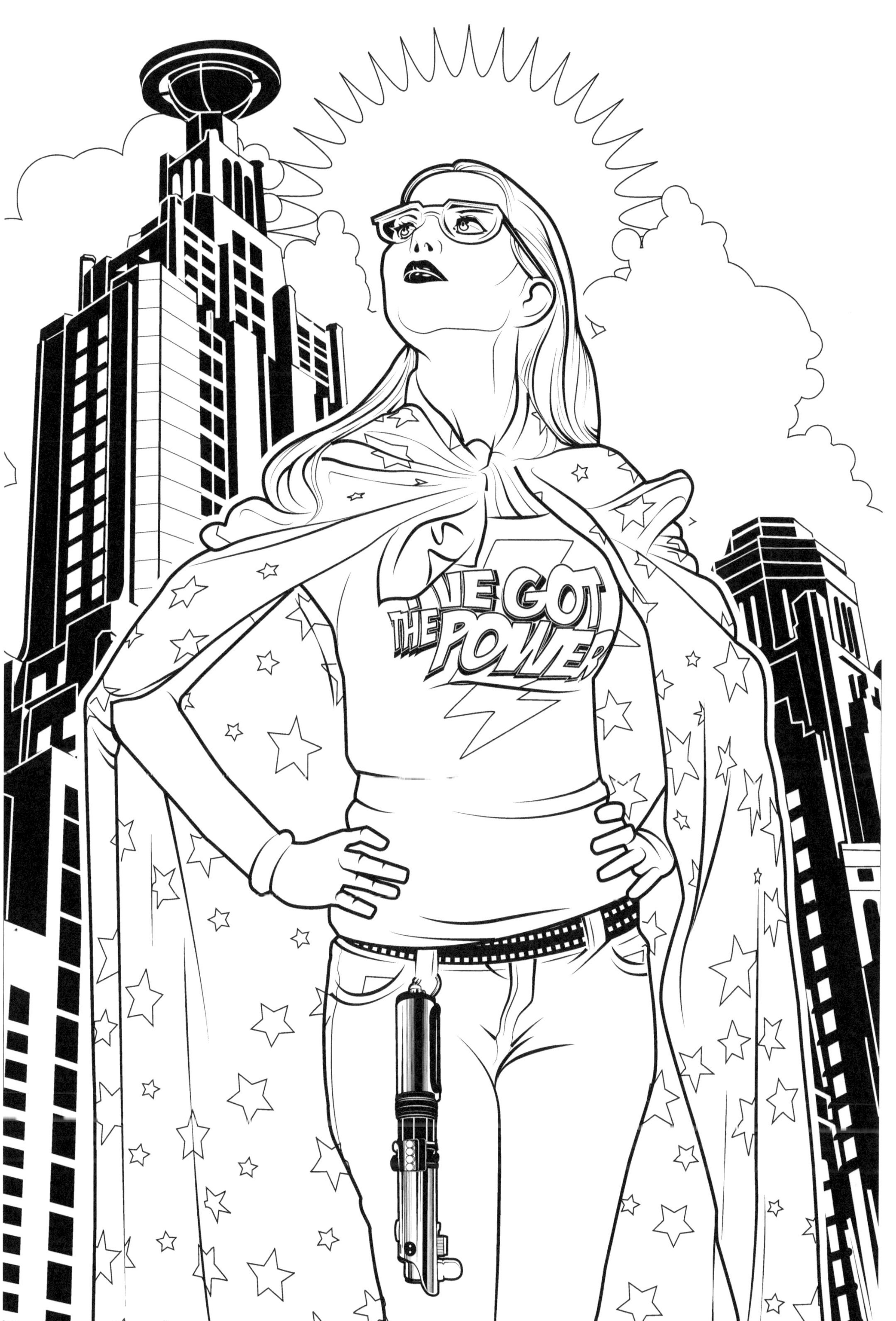
E GOT
THE POWER

No animals were harmed in the
making of this picture.

Choking The Chicken

Model: Kitty Stryker and Heart-On

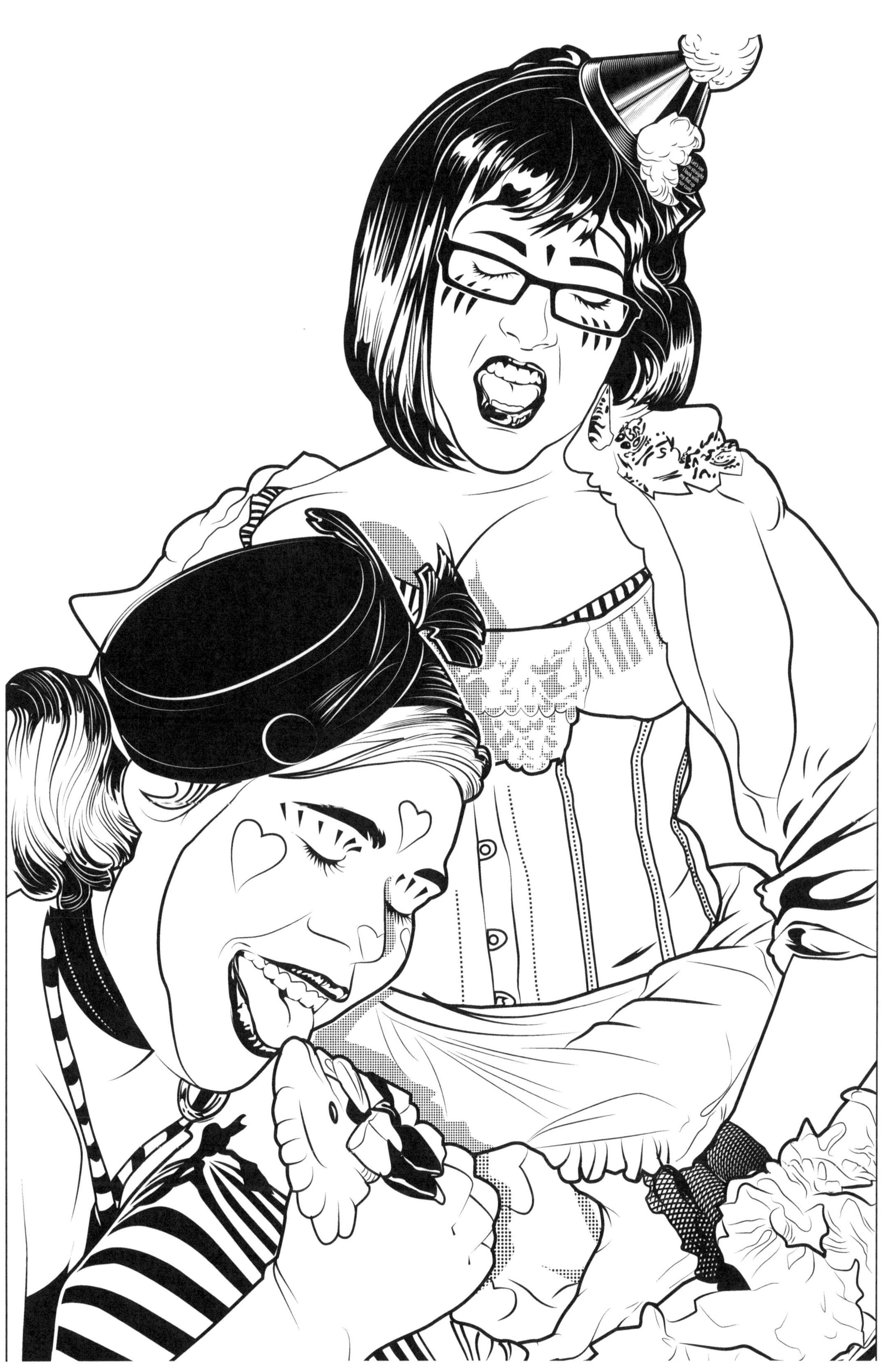
Let's see
ow straight
I look with
my fist up
our cunt

My friend and prop wrangler Jeff Cathcart has proven invaluable in many of my shoots. The toga Scarlet was wearing was really just a satin sheet that Jeff skillfully wrapped around her. The great thing about having a good crew is they bring skills and talents that you don't have. It is often as just fun and exciting working with them as with any of the models.

My Fallen Angel

Model: Scarlet Faux

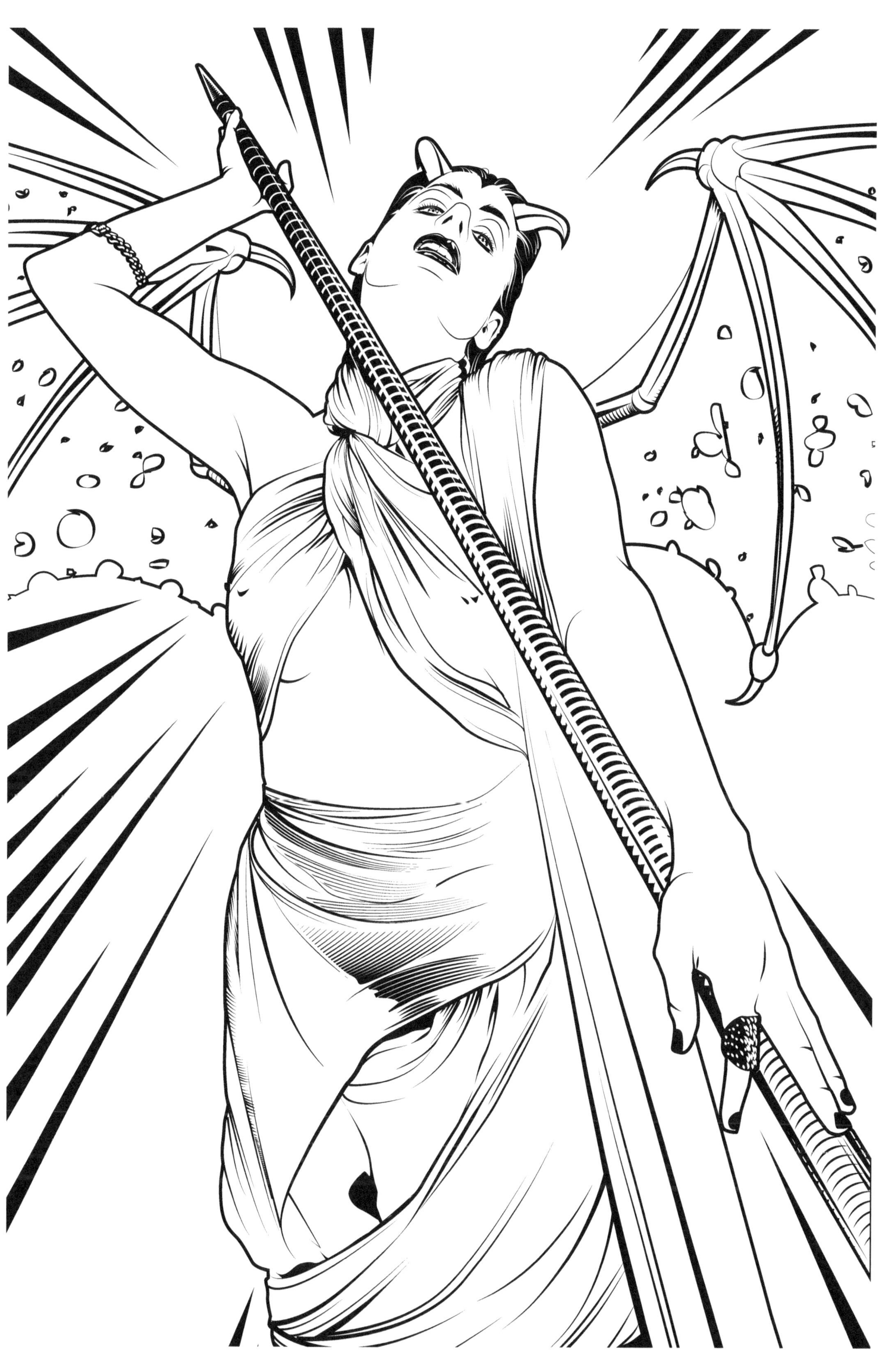

I thought that Libby was a nice, pleasant and professional model to work with. The snake on the other hand was a total Diva!

Tribal Libby

Model: Libby Loo

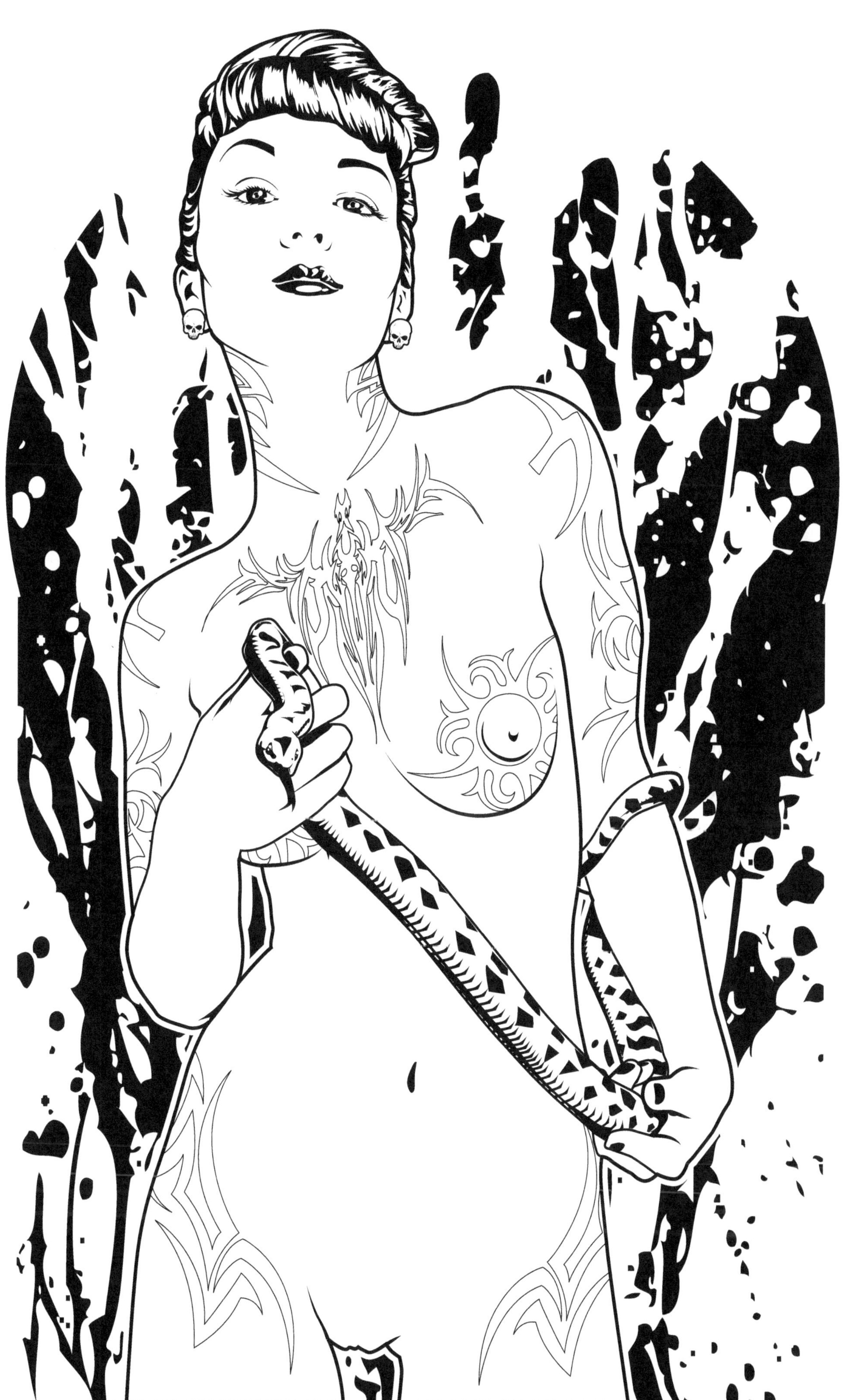

A lady commented after I posted this picture on flickr that she would have fabulous orgasms while riding on a Harley. It has to do with the positioning of your sensitive spots it seems.

Vrrooomm

Model: Raven Le Faye

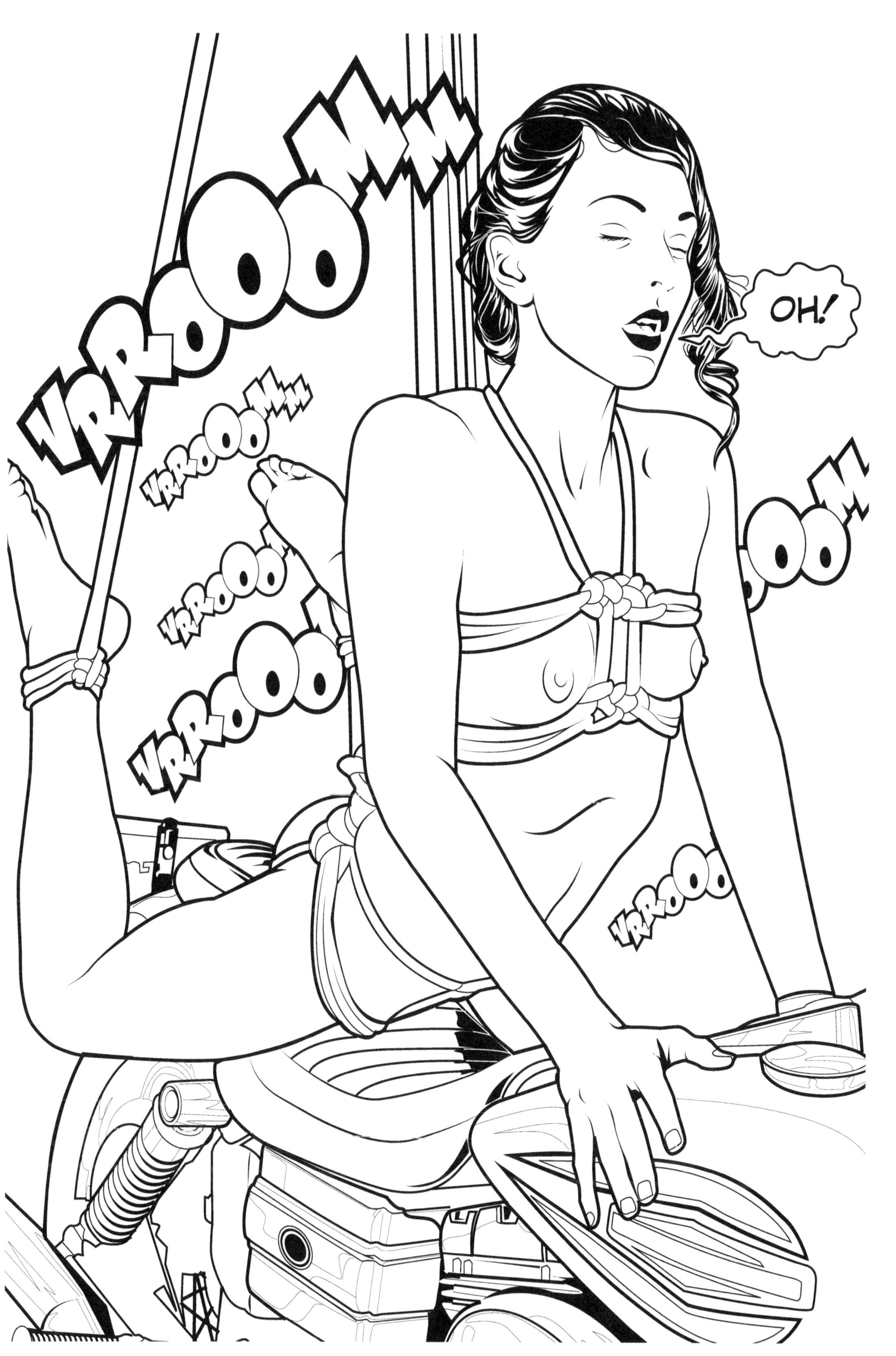

VRROOOMMM
VRROOOMMM
VRROOOM
VRROOO
OH!
OOOM
VRROOO

Are you ready to RUMBLE!

The Wrestler

Model: Cherry Katonic

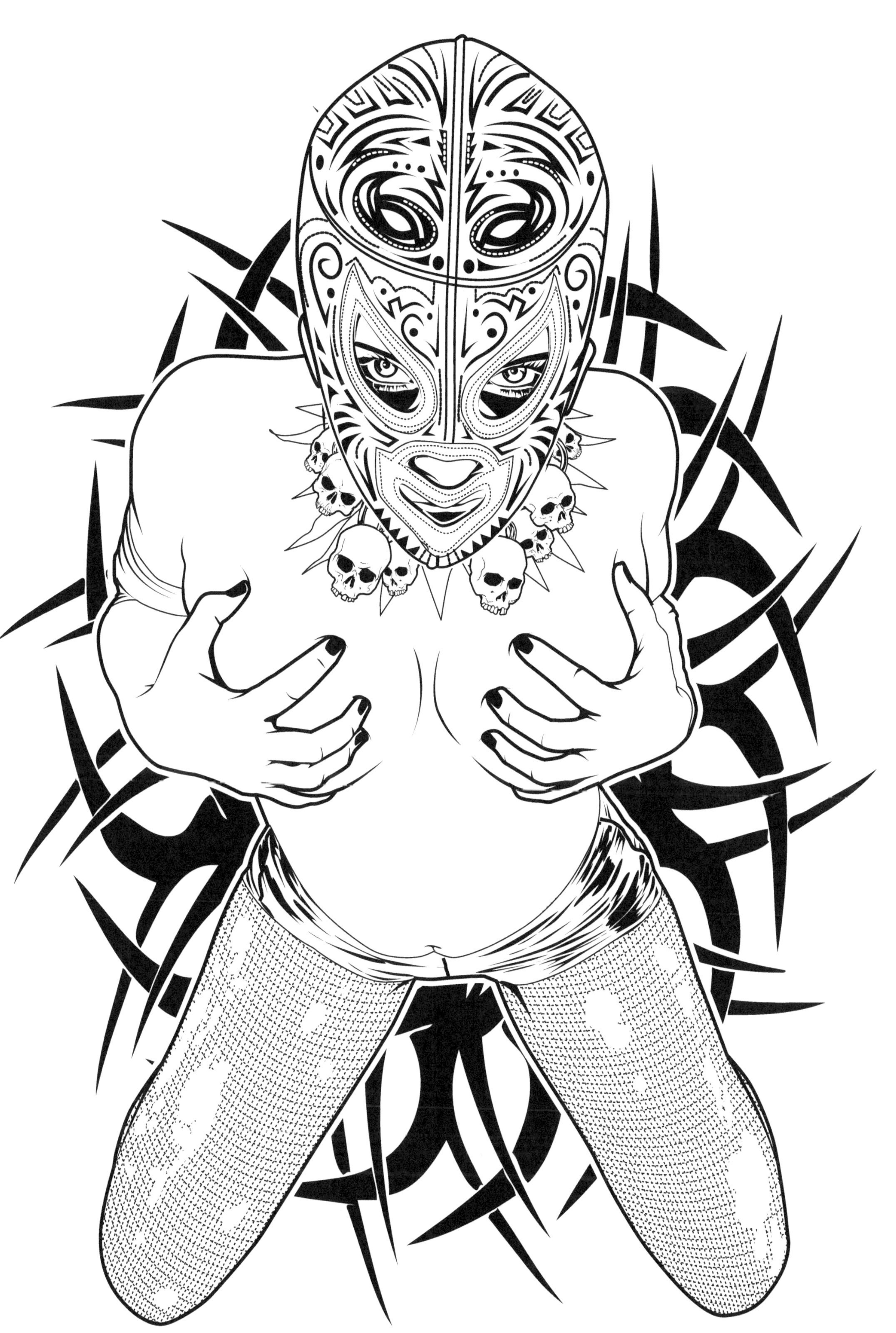

Theirs was a love doomed from the start. He was a married man and she was a member of the Living Dead. In the end the only way she could have him, was to eat him.

Zombie Lovers

Model: Lysa Dazzle and John Walters

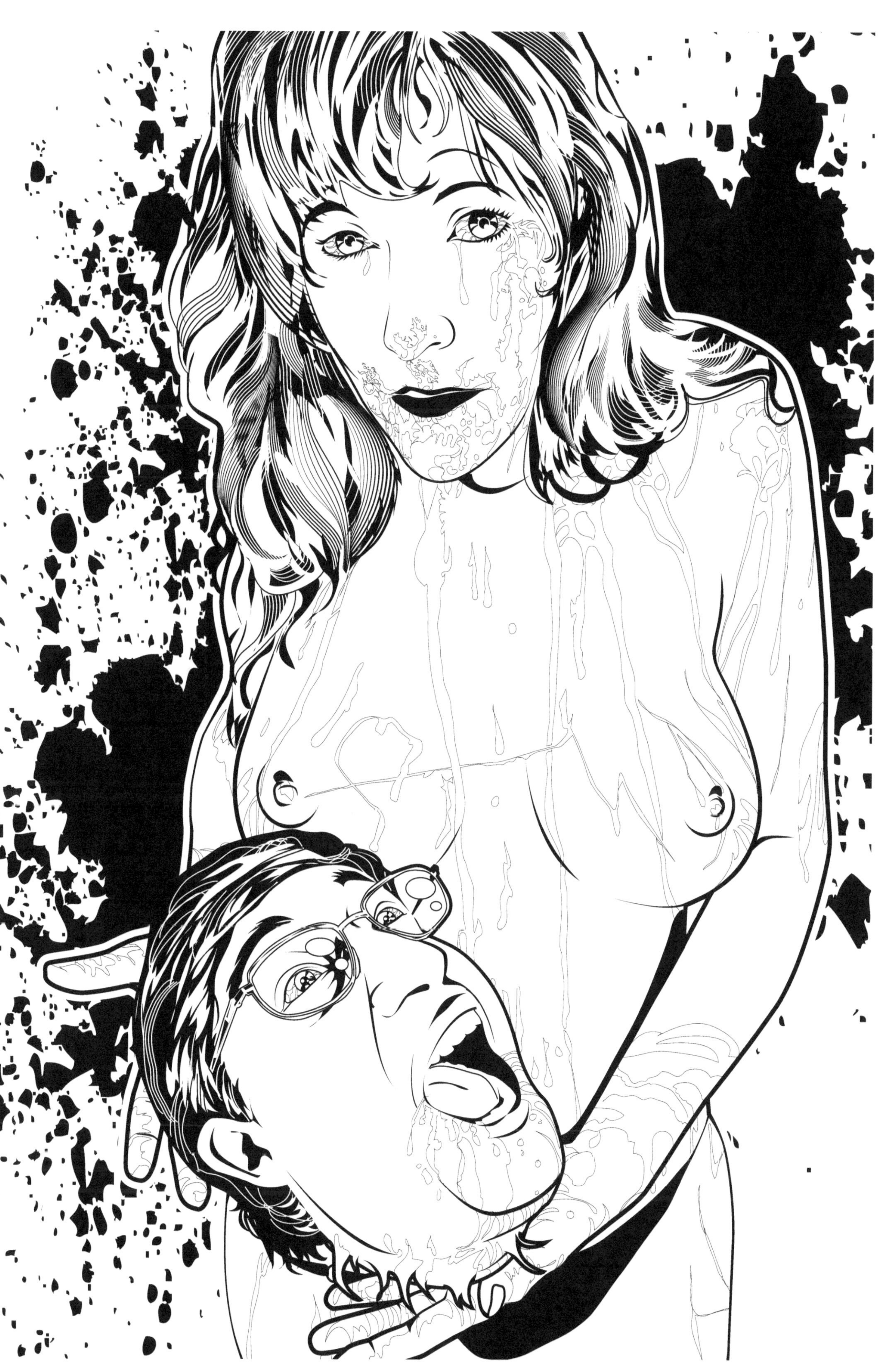

I was at play party in Oakland when I saw a couple I knew were doing some needle play with a friend who had come down from Oregon. Though I didn't bring a camera, (I would never bring a camera to a play party unless it is approved in advance) they asked me to take some shots with one that they had. I snapped off a few good pictures of RedHeadToy. A couple of days later she sent me a few of the shots and gave me permission to do a drawing from one of them for my coloring book. Drawing RedHeadToy looking happy and contented with her needles and feathers, was a nice way to spend a Saturday.

Needle Fairy

Model: RedHeadToy

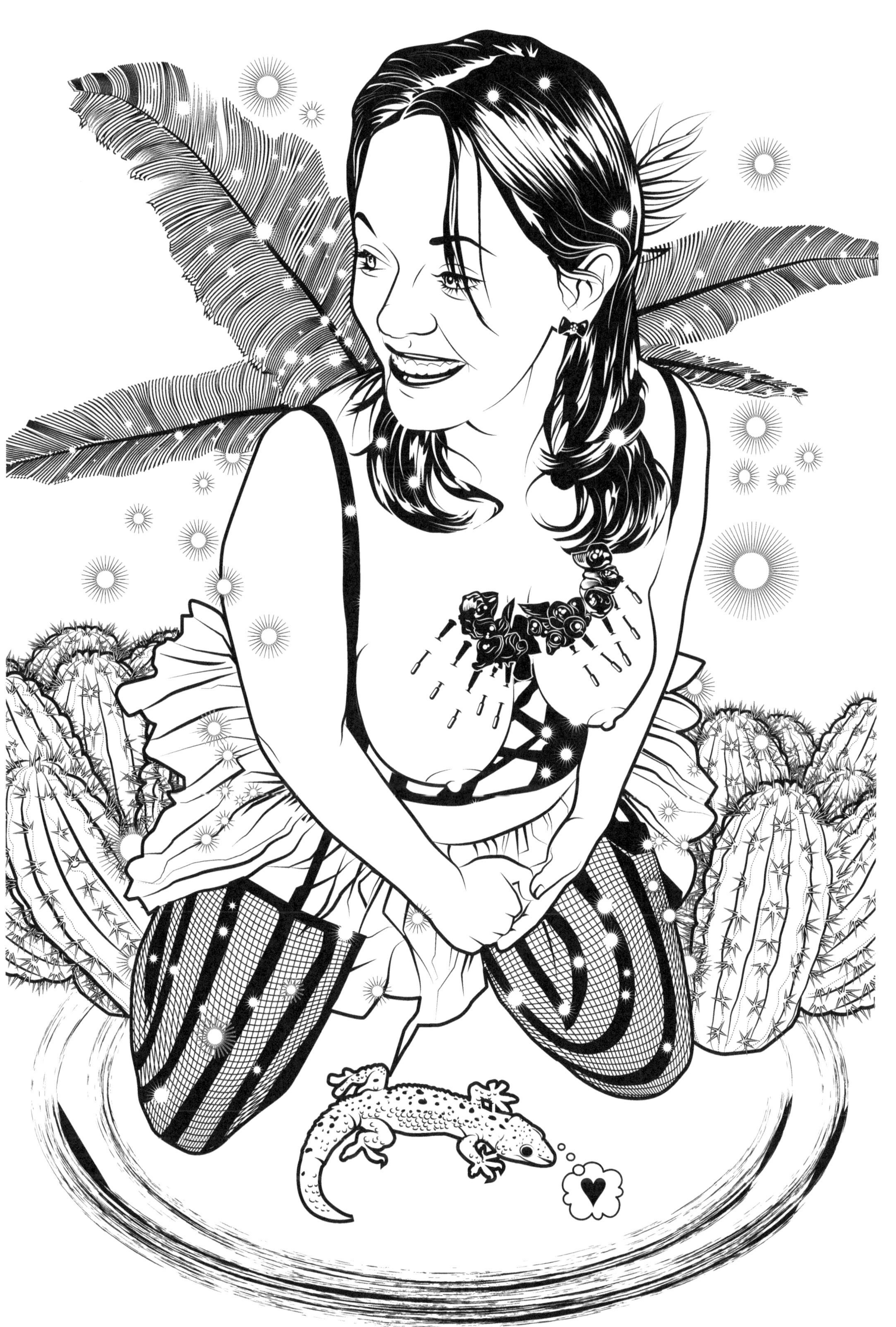

www.ingramcontent.com/pod-product-compliance
Lightning Source LLC
LaVergne TN
LVHW081150110826
845149LV00008B/1615